"You'd have to take me by force," **Randy told him breathlessly.**

"I don't think so," Hawk said, angling his body forward and pressing it suggestively against hers. "I watched you tonight. Right now, your blood is running as hot as mine."

"No."

Her whimpered protest was smothered by his kiss. His lips rubbed against hers until they separated, then claimed her mouth with slow, delicious caresses.

Breathing rapidly, he lifted his lips off hers and opened them against her throat, drawing the fragile, fair skin against his teeth.

Her mind was chanting, no, no, no. But when his mouth returned to claim hers, she responded hungrily. Her hands came up to grasp his thick, dark hair. He slid one hand to the small of her back and pulled her against his hard length.

He groaned. "Why do I want you?"

It was a question she could ask herself. At what point had desire replaced fear? Why did she want to get closer instead of push him away?

He cursed suddenly. "You're my enemy. I hate you. But I want you. . ."

WHAT ARE *LOVESWEPT* ROMANCES?

They are stories of true romance and touching emotion. We believe those two very important ingredients are constants in our highly sensual and very believable stories in the *LOVESWEPT* line. Our goal is to give you, the reader, stories of consistently high quality that may sometimes make you laugh, sometimes make you cry, but are always fresh and creative and contain many delightful surprises within their pages.

Most romance fans read an enormous number of books. Those they truly love, they keep. Others may be traded with friends and soon forgotten. We hope that each *LOVESWEPT* romance will be a treasure—a "keeper." We will always try to publish

LOVE STORIES YOU'LL NEVER FORGET
BY AUTHORS YOU'LL ALWAYS REMEMBER

The Editors

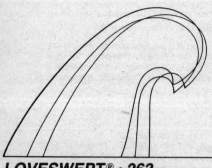

LOVESWEPT® • 263
Sandra Brown
Hawk O'Toole's Hostage

BANTAM BOOKS
TORONTO • NEW YORK • LONDON • SYDNEY • AUCKLAND

HAWK O'TOOLE'S HOSTAGE
A Bantam Book / June 1988

If you would be interested in receiving protective vinyl
covers for your Loveswept books, please write to this address
for information:

Loveswept
Bantam Books
P.O. Box 985
Hicksville, NY 11802

ISBN 0-553-21906-5

Published simultaneously in the United States and Canada

Bantam Books are published by Bantam Books, a division
of Bantam Doubleday Dell Publishing Group, Inc. Its trademark, consisting of the words "Bantam Books" and the
portrayal of a rooster, is Registered in U.S. Patent and
Trademark Office and in other countries. Marca Registrada.
Bantam Books, 666 Fifth Avenue, New York, New York 10103.

PRINTED IN THE UNITED STATES OF AMERICA

O   0 9 8 7 6 5 4 3 2 1

One

They certainly looked like authentic train robbers. From the dusty brims of their hats to the jingling spurs on their boots, they looked as real to Miranda as Butch Cassidy and The Sundance Kid.

To avoid crashing into the temporary barricade of timber piled up on the tracks, the engine had belched a cloud of steam and the train had screeched to a stop. The actors, playing their roles to the hilt, had thundered out of the dense forest lining both sides of the track. The pounding hooves of their horses had plowed up the turf before they reared to a halt beside the tracks. While the well-trained mounts stood at attention, the masked "robbers," with pistols drawn, boarded the train.

"I don't remember reading anything about this in the brochure," a woman passenger remarked uneasily.

" 'Course not, honey. That'd spoil the surprise," her husband said around a chuckle. "Helluva show, isn't it?"

Miranda Price thought so. A helluva show. Worth every penny of the cost of the excursion ticket. The staged holdup had all the passengers enthralled, and none more than Miranda's six-year-old son, Scott. He was sitting beside her on the seat, thoroughly engrossed in the realistic performance. His bright eyes were fixed on the leader of the outlaw band, who was slowly making his way down the narrow aisle of the train while the other bandits stood guard at each end of the car.

"Everybody be calm, stay in your seats, and nobody will get hurt."

He was probably a temporarily unemployed Hollywood actor, or perhaps a stuntman, who had taken this summer job to supplement his fluctuating income. Whatever they were paying him for this job wasn't enough, Miranda thought. He was perfectly suited to the role.

A bandanna covered the lower half of his face, muffling his voice but allowing it to reach every person in the antique railroad car. He was convincingly costumed, wearing a black hat pulled low over his brows, a long white duster, and around his hips a tooled leather gun belt with a thong strapping the holster to his thigh. The holster was empty because he was holding a Colt pistol in his gloved right hand as he moved down the row of seats, carefully scanning each face. His spurs jangled musically with every step.

"Is he really gonna rob us, Mommy?" Scott whispered.

Miranda shook her head no, but didn't take her eyes off the train robber. "It's just make-believe. There's nothing to be afraid of."

But even as she said so, she wasn't certain. Because in that instant the actor's eyes came to rest on her. Sharply, she sucked in her breath. His eyes, white hot and laser bright, pierced straight through her. They were a startling shade of blue, but that alone hadn't taken her breath. If the hostile intensity behind his eyes were part of the act, then his thespian talents were being wasted on this tourist train.

That smoldering gaze remained on Miranda until the man sitting in front of her asked the bandit, "Want us to empty our pockets, gunman?" He was the same man who had reassured his wife earlier.

The robber jerked his stare away from Miranda and looked down at the man. He gave a laconic shrug. "Sure."

Laughing, the tourist stood up and dug into the pockets of his plaid Bermuda shorts. He withdrew a credit card and waved it in front of the masked face. "Never leave home without it," he said in a booming voice, then laughed.

The other tourists on the train laughed with him. Miranda did not. She was looking at the robber. His eyes reflected no humor. "Sit down, please," he said in a whispery voice.

"Aw, say, don't get upset. I've got another pocket." The tourist produced a handful of cash and thrust it at the robber. Without juggling the pistol, he caught the money with his left hand. "There." Smiling broadly, the vacationer looked around for approval and got it from the other passengers. All applauded; some whistled.

The bandit stuffed the cash into the pocket of his duster. "Thanks."

The man sat back down beside his wife, who looked both ill at ease and embarrassed. The man patted her hand. "It's all a gag. Play along, honey."

The robber dismissed them and looked down at

Scott, who was sitting between Miranda and the window. He was staring up at the masked man with awe. "Hello."

"Hello," the boy replied.

"You want to help me make my getaway?"

Innocent eyes opened wider. He flashed the robber a gap-toothed smile. "Sure!"

"Sweetheart," Miranda said cautiously to her son. "I—"

"He'll be all right." The hard stare above the bandanna did nothing to alleviate Miranda's apprehension. If anything it increased it. The cold expression belied the bandit's reassuring words.

He extended his hand to Scott. The boy eagerly and trustingly grasped it. He clambered over his mother's legs and out into the aisle. With Scott preceding the man, they started walking toward the front of the railroad car. Other youngsters aboard the train gave Scott envious looks, while the grown-ups cheered him on.

"See?" the man sitting in front of Miranda said to his wife. "Didn't I tell you it was all a game? They even get the kids involved."

When the outlaw and her son had gone halfway up the aisle, Miranda scrambled out of her seat and started after them. "Wait! Where are you taking him? I'd rather he not get off the train."

The robber spun around and, again, pierced her with his fierce blue eyes. "I told you that he would be all right."

"Where are you going?"

"On a horseback ride."

"Not without my permission, you're not."

"Please, Mommy?"

"Come on, lady, give the kid a break," the obnoxious tourist said. "It's part of the fun. Your kid'll love it."

She ignored him and started up the aisle behind the masked robber, who by now was propelling Scott through the opening at the front of the car. Miranda speeded up. "I asked you not to—"

"Sit down, madam, and keep quiet!"

Stunned by the harsh tone of voice, she spun around. The two robbers who had been guarding the rear entrance of the railroad car had closed in behind her. Above their masks their eyes were wary, nervous, almost fearful, as though she were about to foil a well-orchestrated plan. It was in that instant that Miranda knew this wasn't a game. Not by any means.

Whirling around, she ran up the aisle and launched herself through the door and onto the platform between the passenger car and the engine. Two men, already mounted, were anxiously surveying the area. The robber was hoisting Scott up onto the saddle of his horse.

Scott clutched the horse's thick mane and chattered excitedly, "Gee, he's a big horse. We're up so high."

"Hold on, Scott, and don't let go. That's very important," the bandit instructed him.

Scott!

He knew her son's name.

Acting from the pure maternal instinct to protect her child, Miranda threw herself down the steps. She landed on her hands and knees in the gravel railroad bed, scraping them painfully. The two robbers were beside her in an instant. They grabbed her arms and held her back when she would have run toward Scott.

"Leave her alone," their leader barked. "Mount up. We're getting the hell out of here." The two released her and ran toward their waiting horses. Holding the reins of his horse in one hand and the pistol in the other, the leader said to Miranda, "Get back on the train." He made a jutting motion with his chin.

"Take my son off that horse."

"I told you, he won't be hurt. But you might be if you don't do as I say and get back aboard the train."

"Do what he says, lady."

Miranda turned in the direction of the terrified voice. The engineer of the train was lying facedown in the gravel beside the track. His hands were stacked atop his head. Another of the robbers was keeping him there at gunpoint.

Miranda cried out with fear and anxiety. She ran toward her son, arms outstretched. "Scott, get down!"

"Why, Mommy?"

"Get down this instant!"

"I can't," he wailed. His mother's anxiety had been transmitted to him. His six-year-old mind had suddenly figured out that this was no longer playacting. The small fingers clutching the horse's mane tightened their grip. "Mommy!" he screamed.

The leader hissed a vile curse just as Miranda threw herself against his chest. "Stop anybody who steps off that train," he shouted to his men.

The other passengers, who were by now filling every window on that side of the train, were beginning to panic. Some were shouting advice to Miranda. Others were screaming in fear. Some were too shocked and afraid to say or do anything. Parents were gathering their own children close and holding onto them for dear life.

Miranda fought like a wildcat. Her carefully tended nails became talons, which she would have used to claw the robber's face had she been able to reach it. As it was, his fingers had locked around her wrists like handcuffs. She was no match for his superior strength. She kicked his shins, aimed for his crotch with her knee, and was rewarded with a grunt of pain and surprise when it landed close.

"Let my son go!"

The man in the mask gave her a mighty push that sent her reeling backward. She landed hard on her bottom, but sprang up immediately and tackled him while he had one boot in the stirrup. Catching him off balance, she dug her shoulder into his ribs. She reached for Scott. Scott dived toward her and landed against her chest hard enough to knock the breath out of her. But she held onto him and turned, running blindly. The other bandits were all mounted. Their horses had been made nervous by the shouting. They were prancing around, kicking up clouds of dust that obscured Miranda's vision and clogged her nose and throat.

A thousand pinpricks stabbed her scalp when the robber caught her by the hair and brought her to an abrupt standstill. "Damn you," he cursed behind his mask. "This could have been so easy." She risked letting go of Scott to reach for the bandit's mask. He caught her hand in midair and issued an order in a language she didn't understand. One of his men immediately materialized out of the clouds of swirling dust. "Take the boy. Let him ride with you."

"No!"

Scott was wrestled from Miranda's clutching hands. When the bandit's arm closed around her middle like pincers and he dragged her backward, she fought harder than ever. Digging her heels into the earth, she tried to keep sight of Scott, who was wailing in terror.

"I'll kill you if you hurt my son."

The bandit seemed unfazed by her threat as he mounted his horse and yanked her up with him.

She was still dangling half on, half off the saddle when he spurred the horse. It danced in a tight circle before streaking off through the dense forest. The other riders followed.

The horses' hooves thundered through the otherwise serene woods. They sped through the thick pine forest so fast that Miranda became more afraid of falling off and being trampled than she was of the kidnapper. She clutched his waist in fear that he might let go of her as they began to climb.

Eventually the trees thinned out, but they continued to ride without breaking their speed. The terrain became more rocky. Horseshoes clattered on the rocks, which formed shelves over which they rode. Behind her she could hear Scott crying. If she, an adult, were afraid, what terror must her child be suffering?

After about half an hour they crested a peak, and the band of riders had to reduce their pace to begin their descent of the other side of the mountain. When they reached the first copse of pine along the timberline, the leader slowed his mount to a walk, then came to a full stop. He pressed Miranda's waist with his arm.

"Tell your son to stop crying."

"Go to hell."

"I swear, lady, I'll leave you here for the coyotes to eat," he said in a raspy voice. "You'll never be heard from again."

"I'm not afraid of you."

"You'll never see your son again."

Above the mask, his eyes were icy. Hating them, Miranda reached up and yanked down the bandanna. She had intended to disarm him, but it was she who took a gasping breath.

The rest of his face was as startling as his eyes.

The angles were precise, as though each feature had been lined up with a ruler. His cheekbones were high and as sharp as blades, his jaw perfectly square. His lips were narrow and wide. Above them he had a long, straight nose. He continued to stare at her with open contempt.

"Tell your son to stop crying," he repeated.

The resolve in his voice, in his eyes, chilled her. She would fight him when it was possible to win. Now, her efforts would be futile. She wasn't a coward, but she wasn't a fool either. Swallowing her fear and her pride, she called out shakily, "Scott." When his crying didn't subside, she cleared her throat and tried again, louder this time. "Scott!"

"Mommy?" Scott lowered his grimy hands from his red, weeping eyes and searched her out.

"Don't cry anymore, okay, darling? These . . . these men aren't going to hurt us."

"I wanna go home now."

"I know. So do I. And we will. Shortly. But right now, don't cry, okay?"

The small fists wiped away the remaining tears. He hiccupped a sob. "Okay. But can I ride with you? I'm scared."

She glanced up at her captor. "May he—"

"No." The blunt reply was made before she even finished voicing the question. Ignoring her baleful stare, he addressed his men, giving them orders so that when they urged their mounts forward again, the horse Scott was on was second in the procession. Before nudging his horse, their captor asked her curtly, "Can you ride astride?"

"Who are you? What do you want with us? Why did you take Scott off that train?"

"Throw your right leg over. It'll be safer and more comfortable."

"You know who Scott is. I heard you call him by name. What do you—Oh!"

He slid his hand between her thighs and lifted the right one over the saddle. The leather was warm against her bare skin, but that sensation was mild compared to the feel of his gloved hand on her inner thigh. Before she could recover from that, he lifted her over the pommel and wedged her between it and his open thighs. He flattened his hand against her lower body and pulled her back even farther, until she was snugly pressed against him.

"Stop manhandling me."

"I'm only making it safer for you to ride."

"I don't want to ride."

"You can get down and walk anytime, madam. It wasn't in my plan to bring you along, so if you don't like the traveling accommodations, you've no one to blame but yourself."

"Did you think I would let you take off with my son without putting up a fight?"

His austere face revealed no emotion. "I didn't think about you at all, Mrs. Price."

He flexed his knees and the horse started forward, trailing the others by several yards. Miranda was stunned into silence, not only by the fact that he knew her name, but because while one of his hands was loosely holding the reins of the horse, the other was riding lightly on her hipbone.

"You know me?" She tried not to reveal her anxiety through her voice.

"I know who you are."

"Then you have me at a distinct disadvantage."

"That's right. I do."

She had hoped to weasel out his name, but he lapsed into stoic silence as the horse carefully picked its way down the steep incline. As hazardous as the race up the mountainside had been, traveling down the other side was more so. Miranda expected the horse's forelegs to buckle at any second and pitch them forward. They wouldn't stop rolling until they hit bottom several miles below. She was afraid for Scott. He was still crying, though not hysterically as before.

"That man my son is riding with, does he know how to ride well?"

"Ernie was practically born on a horse. He won't let anything happen to the boy. He's got several sons of his own."

"Then he must understand how I feel!" she cried. "Why have you taken us?"

"You'll know soon enough."

The ensuing silence was rife with hostility. She decided she would say nothing more, not wanting to give him the satisfaction of refusing to answer her.

Suddenly the horse lost its footing. Rocks began to shake loose around them. The frightened animal sought traction, but couldn't find it. He began to skid down the incline. Miranda almost somersaulted over his neck. To prevent that, she clutched the pommel with her left hand. Her right squeezed her captor's thigh. His arm formed a bar as hard as steel across her midriff while, with his other hand, he gradually pulled up on the reins. The muscles in his thighs bunched with the strain of keeping both of them in the saddle until, after what seemed like forever, the horse regained its footing.

Miranda could barely release her pent-up breath for the arm across her diaphragm. He didn't relax his hold until the animal was well under control again. She slumped forward, as if with relief, but all her senses were alert.

When she had reflexively laid her hand on his

thigh, she had inadvertently touched his holster. The pistol was within her grasp! All she had to do was play it cool. If she could catch him off guard, she had a chance of whipping the pistol out of the holster and turning it on him. She could stave off the others while holding their leader at gunpoint long enough for Scott to get on the horse with her. Surely she could find her way back to the train where law enforcement agencies must already be organizing search parties. Their trail wouldn't be difficult to follow, for no efforts had been taken to cover it. They could still be found well before dark.

But in the meantime, she had to convince the outlaw that she was resigned to her plight and acquiescent to his will. Gradually, so as not to appear obvious, she let her body become more pliant against his chest. She ceased trying to maintain space between her thighs and his. She no longer kept her hip muscles contracted, but let them go soft against his lap, which grew perceptibly tighter and harder with each rocking motion of the saddle.

Eventually her head dropped backward onto his shoulder, as though she had dozed off. She made certain he could see that her eyes were closed. She knew he was looking down at her because she could feel his breath on her face and the side of her neck. Taking a deep breath, she intentionally lifted her breasts high, until they strained against her light-weight summer blouse. When they settled, they settled heavily on the arm he still held across her midriff.

But she didn't dare move her hand, not until she thought the moment was right. By then her heart had begun to pound so hard she was afraid he might feel it against his arm. Sweat had moistened her palms. She hoped her hand wouldn't be too slippery to grab the butt of the pistol. To avoid that, she knew she must act without further delay.

In one motion, she sat up straight and reached for the pistol.

He reacted quicker.

His fingers closed around her wrist like a vise and prized her hand off the gun. She grunted in pain and gave an anguished cry of defeat and frustration.

"Mommy?" Scott shouted from up ahead. "Mommy, what's the matter?"

Her teeth were clenched against the pain the outlaw was inflicting on the fragile bones of her wrist, but she managed to choke out, "Nothing, darling. Nothing. I'm fine." Her captor's grip relaxed, and she called to Scott, "How are you?"

"I'm thirsty and I have to go to the bathroom."

"Tell him it's not much farther."

She repeated the dictated message to her son. For the time being Scott seemed satisfied. Her captor let the others go on ahead until the last horse was almost out of sight before he placed one hand beneath her jaw and jerked her head around to face him.

"If you want to handle something hard and deadly, Mrs. Price, I'll be glad to direct your hand to something just as steely and fully loaded as the pistol. But then you already know how hard it is, don't you? You've been grinding your soft little tush against it for the last twenty minutes." His eye darkened. "Don't underestimate me again."

Miranda twisted her head free of his grasp and sat forward on the horse again, keeping her back as rigid and straight as a flagpole. The military posture took its toll quickly. Soon she began to notice a burning sensation between her shoulder blades. It had become almost intolerable by dusk, when they rode out of the woods and into a clearing at the floor of the mountain they had just descended.

Several pickup trucks were parked between a running stream and a burning camp fire. There were men milling around, obviously waiting for their arrival. One called out a greeting in a language Miranda didn't recognize, but that was no surprise. She was unable to concentrate on anything except her discomfort. Fatigue had made her groggy. The situation had taken on a surreal aspect.

That was dispelled the moment the man dismounted and pulled her down to stand beside him. After the lengthy horseback ride, her thighs quivered under the effort of supporting her. Her feet were numb. Before she regained feeling in them, Scott hurled his small body at her shins and closed his arms around her thighs, burying his face in her lap.

She dropped to her knees in front of him and embraced him tightly, letting tears of relief roll down her cheeks. They had come this far and had escaped serious injury. She was grateful for that much. After a lengthy bear hug, she held Scott away from her and examined him. He seemed none the worse for wear, except for his eyes, which were red and puffy from crying. She drew him to her chest again and hugged him hard.

Too soon, a long shadow fell across them. Miranda looked up. Their kidnapper had taken off the white duster, his gloves, his gun belt, and his hat. His straight hair was as inky black as the darkness surrounding them. The firelight cast wavering shadows across his face that blunted its sharp angles but made it appear more sinister.

That didn't deter Scott. Before Miranda realized what he was going to do, the child flung himself against the man. He kicked at the long shins with his tennis shoes and pounded the hard, lean thighs with his grubby fists.

"You hurt my mommy. I'm gonna beat you up. You're a bad man. I hate you. I'm gonna kill you. You leave my mommy alone."

His high, piping voice filled the still night air. Miranda reached out to pull Scott back, but the man held up his hand to forestall her. He endured Scott's ineffectual attack until the child's strength had been spent and the boy collapsed into another torrent of tears.

The man took the boy's shoulders between his hands. "You are very brave."

His low, resonant voice calmed Scott instantly. With solemn, tear-flooded eyes, Scott gazed up at the man. "Huh?"

"You are very brave to go up against an enemy so much stronger than yourself." The others in the outlaw band had clustered around them, but the boy had the man's attention. He squatted down, putting himself on eye level with Scott. "It's also a fine thing for a man to defend his mother the way you just did." From a scabbard attached to his belt, he withdrew a knife. Its blade was short, but sufficient. Miranda drew in a quick breath. The man tossed the knife into the air. It turned end over end until he deftly caught it by the tip of the blade. He extended the ivory handle toward Scott.

"Keep this with you. If I ever hurt your mother, you can stab me in the heart with it."

Wearing a serious expression, Scott took the knife. Ordinarily, accepting a gift from a stranger would have warranted parental permission. Scott, his eyes fixed on the man before him, didn't even glance at Miranda. For the second time that afternoon, her son had obeyed this man without consulting her first. That, almost as much as their perilous situation, bothered her.

Did this pseudo train robber possess supernatural powers? Granted, his manner and voice were seductive. His eyes were unusually blue, but were they truly mesmerizing? Were the men riding with him fellow outlaws or disciples?

She glanced around her. The men had removed their masks, making one thing readily apparent: They were all native Americans. The one referred to as Ernie, whom Scott had ridden with, had long gray hair that had been plaited into two braids, which up till now his hat had kept hidden. His eyes were small, dark, and deeply set; his face was lined and leathery, but there was nothing menacing about him.

In fact, Ernie smiled when her son politely informed his kidnapper, "My name is Scott Price."

"Pleased to meet you, Scott." The man and the boy shook hands. "My name is Hawk."

"Hawk? I never heard that name before. Are you a cowboy?"

Those encircling them snickered, but he answered the question seriously. "No, I'm not a cowboy."

"You're wearing cowboy clothes. You carry a gun."

"Not usually. Just for today. Actually, I'm an engineer."

Scott scratched his grimy cheek where tears had left muddy tracks. "Like on the train?"

"No, not that kind of engineer. A mining engineer."

"I don't know what that is."

"It's rather complicated."

"Hmm. Can I go to the bathroom now?"

"There is no bathroom here. The best we can offer is the woods."

"That's okay. Sometimes Mommy lets me go outside if we're on picnics and stuff." He sounded agreeable enough, but he glanced warily at the wall of darkness beyond the glow of the camp fire.

"Ernie will go with you," Hawk reassured him, pressing his shoulder as he stood up. "When you come back, he'll get you something to drink."

"Okay. I'm kinda hungry, too."

Ernie stepped forward and extended his hand to the boy, who took it without hesitation. They turned and, with the other men, headed toward the camp fire. Miranda made to follow. The man named Hawk stepped in front of her and barred her path. "Where do you think you're going?"

"To keep an eye on my son."

"Your son will be fine without you."

"Get out of my way."

Instead, he clasped her upper arms and walked her backward until she came up against the rough bark of a pine tree. Hawk kept moving forward until his body was pinning hers against the tree trunk. The brilliant blue eyes moved over her face, down her neck, and across her chest.

"Your son seems to think you're worth fighting for." His head lowered, coming closer to hers. "Are you?"

Two

His lips were hard, but his tongue was soft. It made stroking motions against her compressed lips. When they didn't part, he pulled back and looked down into her eyes. Her defiance seemed to amuse rather than anger him.

"You won't get off that easy, Mrs. Price. You deliberately stoked this fire burning in my gut, so now you're going to put it out." He closed his hard fingers around her jaw and prized open her mouth for his questing tongue.

Miranda placed her fists against his muscled chest and put all her strength behind the push, but he wouldn't budge. She was subjected to the most thorough, intimate, rapacious kiss she'd ever had, and there was nothing she could do about it but submit. She was ever mindful of Scott. If their captor turned violent, she wanted him to take his wrath out on her, not her son.

But she didn't capitulate entirely. She squirmed against him, trying to put distance, no matter how slight, between their bodies. However, he seemed to know the softest, most vulnerable spots on her body and adjusted his accordingly while his tongue continued its swirling caress of her mouth.

Miranda finally succeeded in tearing her lips free. "Leave me alone," she said in a low, husky voice. She didn't want Scott to notice them and come charging across the clearing, wielding the knife this barbarian had given him.

"Or else what?" he taunted. He took a strand of her fair hair between his fingers and brushed it across his stern, but sexily damp, mouth.

"Or else I'll take that knife from Scott and stab you in the heart myself."

No smile relieved the austerity of his features, but a facsimile of a laugh rumbled inside his chest. "Because I stole a kiss? It was okay, but hardly worth dying for."

"I didn't ask for a grade."

"If you don't like my kisses, I'd advise you not to try and distract me with your feminine charms again." He slid his hand down her front, covered her breast with his hand and gave it a gentle squeeze. "This is nice, but it's not nice enough to keep me from accomplishing what I set out to do."

She slapped his hand aside. He took a step back, but she knew it was because he chose to and not because she had warded him off. "What have you set out to do?"

"Force the government into reopening the Lone Puma Mine."

His reply was so far removed from what she had expected, she blinked rapidly and wet her lips misapprehensively. In the darkest recesses of her mind, it registered that her lips tasted like a kiss, like a man, like him. But her bewilderment overrode all other thoughts. "Reopening what?"

"The Lone Puma Mine. It's a silver mine. Ever heard of it?" She shook her head. "I'm not surprised. It doesn't seem to be important to anybody but the people who rely on it for their livelihoods. My people."

"*Your* people? The Indians?"

"Good guess," he said sarcastically. "What gave me away? My stupidity or my laziness?"

She had neither done nor said anything to suggest she was a bigot. His reverse snobbery was wholly unjustified, and it caused her temper to snap. "Your blue eyes," she retorted.

"A genetic slip."

"Look, Mr. Hawk, I—"

"Mr. O'Toole. Hawk O'Toole." Again, Miranda blinked at him in confusion. "Another quirk of fate," he said with a dismissive shrug.

"Who are you, Mr. O'Toole?" she asked in a soft voice. "What do you want with Scott and me?"

"My people have worked the Lone Puma Mine for several generations. The reservation is large. We have other means of income, but most of our economy depends on the operation of the mine. I won't bore you with the machinations that took place, but we were swindled out of our ownership."

"So who owns it now?"

"A group of investors. They decided that it wasn't economically feasible to keep it open, so they closed it. Just like that." He snapped his fingers inches in front of her nose. "Without any warning, hundreds of families have been left virtually destitute. And nobody gives a damn."

"What does all that have to do with me?"

"Not a damn thing."

"Then why am I here?"

"I told you before that you were brought along only because you raised such a ruckus."

"But you boarded that train to abduct Scott."

"Yes."

"Why?"

"Why do you think?"

"Obviously to hold him hostage."

He nodded brusquely. "We're holding him for ransom."

"For money?"

"Not exactly."

Enlightenment dawned. "Morton," she whispered.

"That's right. Your husband. He just might get his fellow legislators to listen to him if a band of wild Indians is holding his son hostage."

"He's not my husband any longer."

The blue eyes moved over her caustically. "Yes, I read about your messy divorce in the newspapers. Representative Price divorced you because you were unfaithful to him." He leaned forward again, pressing her against the tree and nudging her body suggestively. "From the way you were snuggling against my fly on our way here, I can see how he's well rid of a wife like you."

"Keep your filthy opinions of me to yourself."

"You know," he said, reaching up and running his index finger along her jaw, "for a hostage, you're awfully high and mighty."

She jerked her head away from his touch. "And you're a fool. Morton won't lift a finger to get me back."

"Undoubtedly. But we've got his son too."

"Morton knows that Scott is safe as long as he's with me."

"Then maybe we ought to separate you. Or send you back and keep the boy." He carefully gauged her reaction. "Even in the firelight I can see how much that idea frightens you. Unless you want that to happen, you'd be smart to do as you're told."

"Please," she begged shakily, "don't hurt Scott. Don't keep us apart. He's just a little boy. He'll be afraid unless I'm in sight."

"I have no plans to injure either you or Scott. Yet," he added menacingly. "Just do as I say at all times. Do we have an understanding, Mrs. Price?"

As hateful as it was to comply, that was the safest tack to take for the time being. She nodded.

Hawk stepped aside and motioned with his head for her to precede him toward the camp fire. Over her shoulder she asked him, "Aren't you afraid the fire will be spotted? They're bound to be looking for us by now."

"Since that is a likelihood, we've made provisions for it."

She followed the direction of his gaze. All the horses had been unsaddled and were being loaded into a long trailer.

"We'll erase their hoof marks and the trailer tire tracks. If anyone happens upon us tonight, they'll find a group of inebriated Indian fishermen who can't hold up their britches, much less a train full of tourists."

"Except that I'll be here screaming my lungs out for help," she said smugly.

"We've made provision for that, too."

"Like what?"

"Chloroform."

"You would chloroform us?"

"If the need arises," he said offhandedly, before sauntering away and calling out an order for the men to speed up the loading process and get the trailer on its way.

Miranda fumed over how negligently he turned

his back on her, obviously considering her nothing more than a nuisance, certainly not a threat. Stung by his casual disregard, she went in search of Scott and found him devouring a plate of canned beans and Spam. "This is good, Mommy."

"I'm glad you're enjoying it." Nervously, she glanced at Ernie, who was sitting cross-legged beside her son. She hesitantly lowered herself to a fallen log and sat down.

"Would you like some food?" the Indian asked her.

"No, thank you. I'm not hungry." He merely shrugged and kept on eating.

"Guess what, Mommy? Ernie said that tomorrow I can ride on the horse again, only this time by myself, if I'm careful to hold on. He said his little boy will teach me how. I'm going to visit their house. They don't have a VCR, but I said that's okay 'cause they have horses. And a goat too. I'm not scared of goats, am I? Ernie said they don't hurt you, but sometimes they chew on your clothes."

She wanted to shout at him, to remind him of the danger they were in, but she caught herself just in time. Scott was only a child. His innocence of the gravity of their situation was his protection from it. Hawk O'Toole hadn't threatened either Scott or her with physical injury or death. He seemed certain that Morton would respond favorably to his demands. She dared not think of what would happen to Scott and her if he didn't.

Shortly afterward, the loaded horse trailer lumbered out of the clearing and disappeared down a dirt road. Using blankets, the men whisked away its tracks, until all that was left were the tire tracks of the pickup trucks parked nearby.

After taking several swigs apiece of cheap whiskey, they sprinkled it on their clothes. The clearing began to smell like a disreputable tavern. They jokingly practiced walking and talking drunk. After everyone had eaten, they sat around the camp fire, chatting companionably, smoking, and preparing their bedrolls for the night. They hardly looked or acted like hardened criminals who just that afternoon had committed a federal offense.

When Hawk got around to noticing Scott and her again, the child was leaning heavily against her arm. "He's exhausted," she said haughtily. She disliked having to look up Hawk's tall, lean body in order to address him face-to-face. "Where will we be sleeping?"

"In the back of that pickup." He pointed it out to her and reached for her arm to help her to her feet. She rudely refused his assistance and stood up on her own. He bent down and lifted Scott into his arms.

"I'll carry him," Miranda said quickly.

"*I'll* carry him."

His long stride covered the distance much faster than hers. He had already deposited the boy in a sleeping bag in the back of the pickup by the time she caught up with him.

"Can I say my prayers now?" Scott asked around a broad yawn.

"I think you're too sleepy tonight. Why don't you just say them in your heart?"

"Okay," he mumbled. "Gee, Mommy, look how many stars there are."

She looked above her and was startled to see a velvet-black sky studded with brilliant stars. They looked enormous and close enough to touch. "They're beautiful, aren't they?"

"Uh-huh. I think this is where God lives. 'Night, Mommy. 'Night, Hawk."

Scott rolled to his side, drew his knees to his

chest, and was instantly asleep. Dangerously close to tears, Miranda pulled the sleeping bag over his shoulders and tucked it beneath his chin. When she turned around and faced Hawk, her eyes were glittering with determination. "If you hurt him, I'll kill you."

"So you've said. And as I've said, it's not my intention to hurt him."

"Then what's all this for?" she cried, spreading her arms wide at the sides of her body. "Where's your bargaining power?"

"I won't hurt him," he said softly, "but he might never go home again. If your ex-husband doesn't come through for us, we just might keep Scott with us forever."

Issuing a growl of hatred, Miranda threw herself against him, claws bared. She scratched the side of his face and watched as slender threads of blood formed on his hard cheek. Her triumph was short-lived. Hawk caught her arm and forced it behind her, cramming her hand high, until it lay between her shoulder blades. The pain was immense, but she didn't utter a single sound. She gritted her teeth against it. The tussle had alerted the others. They emerged from the darkness, ready to do their leader's bidding.

"It's all right," Hawk said, releasing her suddenly. "It's just that Mrs. Price doesn't like me."

"Are you sure?" Ernie asked around a laugh. He added something in his native language that caused all the men to laugh uproariously. Hawk glanced down at her. He snatched a blanket from the ground and ungraciously tossed it to her.

"Get into the truck and cover up with this."

Her pride was smarting as much as her arm . . . and her saddle-sore thighs and buttocks. She folded the blanket around her and clumsily climbed onto the tailgate. As she was doing so, Ernie made another comment that caused an outburst of masculine laughter, louder than the one before.

Having no doubt that whatever he had said was crude and in reference to her, she lay down beside Scott and squeezed her eyes shut. She listened as the men shuffled back to their sleeping bags around the camp fire. She supposed she should be grateful that Scott and she had the pickup between them and any wildlife that might come prowling during the night, but the corrugated metal didn't make a very comfortable bed. She wiggled inside the blanket, trying in vain to find a softer spot.

"We only have enough sleeping bags for the men."

Her eyes popped open. She was alarmed to see Hawk standing beside the truck, watching her. He had blotted the blood from his face, but her scratches were still obvious. "Not enough for squaws, I guess."

"Not enough for an extra hostage we didn't count on having along."

"What did he say?"

"Who? Oh, Ernie?" His eyes moved down to her chest. "In so many words, he said you either liked me a lot or you were cold."

The shorts and top she had dressed in that morning were suited to a sunny summer afternoon spent in the foothills, but not for the late-season evening air at this elevation. Her skin was covered with gooseflesh. That wasn't what he was referring to. It was the distinct impressions her nipples were making against her blouse. A tide of heat washed through her, warming her momentarily, but doing nothing to relax her nipples, which still held Hawk's attention.

"I believed the latter to be true." He extended his hand and brushed his knuckles back and forth across one of the sensitive tips. "However, if my guess was wrong, I'd be happy to give you something else." His voice was as rough as the bark of the pine tree he'd sandwiched her against earlier, but as soft as the wind soughing through the needles of the upper branches.

Miranda shrank from his erotic touch. "What else did he say?" she asked through lips that had gone stiff and wooden.

Hawk withdrew his hand, but not his captivating blue gaze. "He said that I would sleep a lot warmer if I stayed with the blanket. On the other hand," he added, touching his scratched cheek, "he said I might not get any sleep at all."

She shot him a venomous look and pulled the blanket up to her earlobes, closing her eyes so she wouldn't have to look at his sardonic expression. She let a long while pass before she opened her eyes again. When she did, he was gone, though she hadn't heard a sound or felt any movement in the air. She wondered how long he had stood there staring at her before he moved away.

She listened, but all she could hear was the crackling and popping of burning firewood and Scott's soft, regular snores. Drawing comfort and faith from that sweet, familiar sound, she miraculously fell asleep.

Three

One moment she was asleep and alone. The next, she was awake and he was with her. Like liquid mercury, he soundlessly and heavily spread over her body to completely cover her. One of his hands closed over her mouth, the other held the tip of a knife at her throat. Into her ear he whispered roughly, "If you even breathe loud, I'll kill you."

She believed him.

Through the darkness, his eyes gave off an icy cold, unfeeling light. She made a slight bobbing motion of her head, indicating that she understood him. But he didn't relax his hand over her mouth. If anything, she felt his muscles grow more taut.

The reason became obvious seconds later when she heard the sound of a vehicle approaching the clearing from the uneven dirt road. A pair of headlights arced across the encircling trees. Dust swirled when the driver braked. Doors were pushed open.

"Stand up and put your hands in the air."

The military sharpness of the command startled Miranda. Her eyes sprang wide as she gazed up at

Hawk. He was mouthing swearwords. He feared the same thing she did, that the voices would awaken Scott.

She fervently prayed that he would sleep through this. If he woke up and started crying, there was no telling what might happen. He could be struck by a stray bullet during a shoot-out between his kidnappers and his rescuers. Or Hawk might realize that he had failed in his mission and, since he had nothing to lose, take everybody else down with him.

She looked at the man lying on top of her. Could he murder a child in cold blood? Focusing on the stern, hard, uncompromising line of his mouth, she came to the bone-chilling decision that he could.

Please, Scott, please don't wake up.

"Who are you and what are you doing here?"

Hawk's men had apparently been handpicked for their acting abilities. They pretended to have just been awakened from drunken stupors, though Miranda knew that if Hawk had been alerted to the approach of a vehicle, the others also must have been. They appeared to be bemused and befuddled by the officers' terse interrogation and stammered nonsensical answers to each question. Eventually the lawmen lost patience with them.

"For heaven's sake, they're just a bunch of drunk Indians," one said to the other. "We're wasting our time here."

Miranda felt every muscle in Hawk's body quiver with fury. Close to her eyes, a vein in his temple ticked with rage.

"Did you see anybody on horseback today? Six or seven riders?" one of the officers asked the group. "They would have come from that direction."

There was a brief conversation between the Indians in their own language before some of them indicated to the officers that they hadn't seen any horseback riders.

One of the officers let out a deep breath. "Well, much obliged. Keep your eyes open, will ya? And report anything that looks fishy."

"Who are you looking for?"

Miranda recognized Ernie's voice, though he was deliberately sounding naive and humble.

"A lady and a kid. They were kidnapped off the Silverado excursion train today by a gang of horsemen."

"What did these horsemen look like?" Ernie asked. "What should we be watching for?"

"They were wearing bandannas over their faces, but it was a shifty and mean bunch from what folks on the train said. The leader stole some money from one of the passengers, ripped it right out of his hands. Hear tell the woman put up a helluva fight to protect her kid when they dragged him off the train. But the big one, the leader that is, snatched her up, too, and rode off with her. Can't say I blame him," he added on a lewd laugh. "They're passing her picture around for identification. She's a looker. Blonde, green-eyed."

Hawk glanced down at Miranda. She averted her eyes.

Good-byes were said. The car doors were slammed shut. The headlights swept the clearing again. Dust rose, then settled again with a ponderous silence. Eventually even the car's motor could no longer be heard.

"Hawk, they're gone."

Hawk removed his hand from Miranda's mouth, but he didn't lever himself up. He stared down at her lips. They were white and still. He stroked them with his thumb, as though to rub some color back into them.

"Hawk?"

"I hear you," he shouted impatiently.

For several seconds there was a tense silence around the smoldering remnants of the camp fire. Gradually, sounds of resettlement could be heard. Then more silence. Still, Hawk remained where he was.

He eased the knife away from her throat. When she saw the razor sharpness of the blade, her eyes flashed with anger. "You could have killed me with that thing," she hissed.

"If you had given us away, I would have."

"What about Scott? If he had woken up and started crying, would you have killed him?"

"No. He's an innocent." He thrust his body upward, wedging his knee between hers and parting her thighs. "But everybody in the state knows you're not innocent. You heard the man; you're a looker. How many lovers did you seduce before your husband finally had all the unfaithfulness he could stomach and dumped you?"

"Get off me."

He looked at her through narrowed eyes. "I thought you would like it."

"Well, I don't. I don't like you. You're a thief and a kidnapper and—"

"Not a thief."

"You took money from that man on the train at gunpoint."

"He offered it to me, remember? I didn't steal it."

"But you'll spend it."

"Damn right I will," he said. "I'll consider it a gift from the haves to the have-nots."

"Oh, spare me. How do you see yourself? A twentieth-century Robin Hood? You're wrong. You're a criminal. Nothing more."

Wanting to shove him away, she placed her hands on his shoulders. That proved to be a mistake. His shoulders were bare and smooth. So was his chest. Shirtless, it was a sleek, supple expanse of bronzed skin, uninterrupted except for the disks of deeper color around his distended nipples.

Quelling an urge to run her palms over him, she tried to push him away. He lowered his head and nestled it in the hollow between her neck and shoulder. He sank his fingers into her hair. They enfolded her scalp and held her head still. He caught her earlobe between his strong, white teeth and flicked it with his tongue.

"Don't," she said breathlessly.

"Why not? Nervous? First time you've ever had it from an Indian, Mrs. Price?"

She was unable to think of an insult scathing enough for him. "If it weren't for Scott, I'd—"

"What? Give in? Take me right here? Does it bother you that your son is sleeping close by? Is that what's making you resist?"

"No! Stop this," she cried out softly.

"Oh, I get it. This is part of the making-it-with-a-savage fantasy. You resist and I overpower you. Is that how the game is played?"

"Don't, please. Please."

"Good. That's good. You can tell all your friends I forced myself on you. That makes for much more scintillating parlor conversation."

He stroked her lips with his tongue. Reflexively, her hands squeezed his shoulders. Her back arched, forcing her body up against his. "Good, you're warm," he said, groaning as he nuzzled the cleft of her thighs with his lower body. "I'll bet you're wet, too."

Then he kissed her, sending his tongue deeply, sensuously into her mouth while his hips rhythmically massaged her middle.

"Hawk?"

His head snapped up and he swore viciously. "What?"

"You said to rouse you at dawn." Ernie's voice came to them from out of the darkness, which was beginning to have blurred edges of gray. He sounded apologetic.

Hawk's eyes probed Miranda's as he eased himself up. Looming above her, he surveyed her mussed hair, kiss-rouged lips, splayed limbs. "Just as the news stories suggested, Mrs. Price, you are a slut. It's a good thing we kidnapped Scott. Ransoming you wouldn't bring us a plugged nickel."

He vaulted over the side of the pickup and walked away, hiking up the jeans he had hastily pulled on but left unfastened. Miranda's eyes smarted with tears of resentment and outrage. She blotted them out of her eyes. Using a corner of the scratchy wool blanket, she tried to scrub the taste of Hawk O'Toole's kisses off her lips.

But she wasn't very successful.

"Wake up, Randy. We're here."

Miranda's shoulder was given a hard shake. She raised her head from where it had been resting against the passenger-side window of the pickup truck. The awkward position had resulted in a crick in her neck. She rolled her head around her shoulders several times to work out the stiffness.

Blinking her eyes open, she looked across at the man sitting behind the steering wheel. Suddenly she realized they were the only two in the truck.

Alarmed, she cried out, "Scott!" She reached for the
door handle, but Hawk's hand whipped out and
grabbed her wrist before she could cannonball out
the door.

"Relax. He's with Ernie. There."

He pointed through the bug-splattered windshield.
Scott was trotting behind Ernie like a trusting puppy.
They were making their way along a path leading to
a mobile home.

"Scott said he had to go to the bathroom, so I told
him to go on ahead." Hawk unfolded a newspaper
and slapped the front page with his fingertips. "You
made headlines, Randy."

"Why are you calling me that?"

"That's how you're referred to in the papers. Why
didn't you tell me that's what you're called?"

"You didn't ask."

"Was that your husband's pet name for you?"

"No, I grew up with it."

"I thought your reputation as an easy lay might
have earned you the nickname."

She didn't waste her breath on a comeback. Instead she scanned the headlines. The stories of the
kidnapping had been written according to eyewit-
ness accounts. After clearing the barricade off the
tracks with the assistance of several passengers, the
engineer had returned the train to the station. He
had radioed ahead of their arrival. The FBI, along
with state and local law enforcement agencies, had
been there to meet the train. Obviously, the media
had been well represented too.

"Your ex was waiting for the train at the depot.
He's all shook up."

The front page carried a picture of State Representative Morton Price. In the candid photograph,
his handsome face was twisted into a grimace of

anguish. He was quoted as saying, "I'll do anything, *anything,* to get my son Scott back. Randy, too, of course."

She laughed bitterly. "He's not breaking habit."

"Meaning?"

"He's milking the publicity for all it's worth. And as usual, I'm an afterthought."

"Do you expect me to sympathize?"

She gave him a level look. "I don't expect you to do anything but act like a bastard. So far, you haven't disappointed me, Mr. O'Toole."

"I don't intend to." He opened his door and stepped out. When Randy joined him on the other side of the truck, he made a sweeping gesture with his hand. "Welcome."

She gazed around her at the village. It was comprised mostly of mobile homes, although there were several permanent dwellings built of either adobe or wood. The one main street was deserted. There was a building that served as gas station, grocery store, and post office, but there was no one about. Another building looked like it might be a school, but its doors were locked. Beyond that, there wasn't much to see. Her eyes were drawn to the rocky road that snaked up the hillside until it disappeared over the crest.

"The mine?" Randy asked, nodding in that direction.

"Yes." He gazed down at her with a cynical expression. "The town isn't quite what you're accustomed to, is it?"

She chose not to pick up the gauntlet. "My estimation of your town will vastly improve if you'll direct me to a bathroom."

"I think Leta will make hers available to you."

"Leta?" Miranda fell into step beside him.

"Ernie's wife. And you can forget about trying to make a phone call. They don't have a telephone."

A telephone pole was the first thing Randy had looked for. She hadn't seen one. Almost as irksome as that was Hawk's ability to read her mind.

A goat, tethered to a stake, glared at them as they crossed the dusty yard and went up the concrete steps. Hawk knocked once, then pushed open the door to the mobile home. The aroma of cooking food made Randy's stomach growl. Once her eyes had adjusted to the dimness, she saw her son sitting at the table. With a lamentable shortage of table manners, he was shoveling food into his mouth from the plate in front of him.

"Hey, Mommy, did you see Geronimo? That's the goat's name. This is Donny, my new friend. He's *seven.* This is Leta."

Randy acknowledged the introductions. Donny glanced away shyly. Leta, after staring at the scratches on Hawk's cheek, gazed at her with unabashed curiosity. Randy was shocked to see that Ernie's wife was not only much younger than he, but younger than Randy herself.

"Would you like some food?" the young woman asked her. "It's just hash, but—"

"Yes, please." Randy smiled at her pleasantly. Leta stopped nervously wringing her hands and returned the smile.

"I'm sure Mrs. Price is hungry," Hawk said, as he threw his long leg over the seat of a chair and straddled it, sitting in it backward. "She must have been expecting buffalo jerky and fry bread for breakfast. When we offered to buy her an Egg McMuffin, she turned us down flat."

Ernie chuckled. Leta looked confused. Randy ignored him. To Leta she said, "May I use your bathroom, please?"

"Yes, of course. It's down the hall."

Hawk shot up. "I'll show her where it is."

Randy went through the kitchen and into the narrow hallway leading to the back of the home. Hawk reached around her and opened the bathroom door. He peered around it and gave the cubicle a cursory inspection.

"What did you expect to find?"

"A window you might possibly squeeze through."

She made an impatient sound and tried to step around him. He remained where he was. "Going in with me?" she asked sweetly.

"I don't think that's necessary, but I'll be on the other side of this door."

She propped her hands on her hips. "Maybe you should search me."

The clear eyes traveled down her body and back up again. "Maybe I should."

The heel of his hand gave her shoulder a slight push and her back landed against the wall. Before she could stave them off, his hands disappeared beneath the hem of her blouse. They moved over the lacy cups of her bra, kneading her breasts quickly and lightly. From there his hands moved to her back, running up and down her skin. At her front again, he unsnapped the waistband of her shorts and, flattening his hand, slid it down over her belly, then around to her hips where he palmed her derriere.

"Nothing there that shouldn't be," he said calmly, when he withdrew his hands.

Randy was too shocked to say anything. She only gaped at him breathlessly. Her face had gone pale, though blood was pumping through her system in hot, rapid jets.

"Don't ever dare me," he warned softly. "Not even by implication. I'll call your bluff every time." He gave her a gentle shove into the bathroom and closed the door.

Randy leaned against the door for support until she had regained her breath. She was trembling. At the basin, she turned on the taps and cupped several handfuls of water, scooping them up to her flushed face. After she had blotted it dry, she looked at her reflection in the mirror.

It was a sad sight. Her hair was a mess. It was littered with twigs and leaves, leftovers of the breakneck ride through the forest. Her clothes were dirty. Her makeup was more than twenty-four hours old.

"Ravishing," she said dryly. Then, remembering that she had almost been ravished, she frowned.

Taking up a bar of soap, she vigorously washed off her stale makeup. Using a finger, she brushed her teeth. Carefully, she picked the forest debris from her hair and worked through the stubborn tangles with her fingers. After using the toilet and brushing off her clothes as best she could, she left the bathroom.

Hawk wasn't waiting outside the door for her after all. He was sitting at the kitchen table, drinking a beer and talking softly with Ernie. He had subjected her to the "search" merely to insult her, not because he really feared that she would escape. When they noticed her standing in the doorway, the conversation came to an abrupt halt.

"Where's Scott?"

"Outside."

She checked the window. Scott was warily petting Geronimo while Donny encouraged him not to be afraid. Satisfied that he was in no immediate danger, she turned back toward the table and sat down in the chair Leta pointed out to her. It was midafternoon, an unusual time for a meal. She had been offered breakfast as soon as they had left the campsite early that morning, but she had declined. They hadn't stopped for lunch, so she ate all the food Leta put on her plate. The cup of coffee that followed it was strong, hot, and restorative.

She sipped it, then looked across the table at Hawk and asked bluntly, "What do you intend to do with us?"

"Hold you hostage until your husband—*ex*-husband—gets a guarantee from the governor that the mine will be reopened."

"That could take months of negotiation," she cried, aghast.

Hawk shrugged. "Maybe."

"Scott is supposed to start school in a few weeks."

"School just might have to start without him. Don't you have confidence in your husband's powers of persuasion?"

"Why don't you simply ask for money like an ordinary kidnapper?"

His expression hardened. Ernie cleared his throat and stared down at his hands. Leta fidgeted in her chair.

"If we wanted a handout, Mrs. Price," Hawk said coldly, "we could all live on welfare."

She could have kicked herself for making the thoughtless outburst. It had damaged Hawk's pride. His blue eyes might contradict his Indian heritage, but his fierce pride certainly didn't.

She took a calming breath. "I don't see how you plan to pull this off, Mr. O'Toole. Negotiating with any government involves miles of red tape. Morton probably won't be able to get an appointment with the governor for weeks."

Hawk thumped the newspaper that was now folded and lying on the table. "This will help, just as we planned. Your husband is running for reelection. He's already news. The kidnapping of his child puts him in the forefront of everybody's mind. Public pressure alone will force Governor Adams to meet our demands."

"You've apparently thought it out carefully. How did you know Scott and I would be on the Silverado train?"

She could tell instantly that her innocent question struck a nerve. Ernie and Leta looked uneasily at Hawk, who recovered quickly and answered, "A kidnapper makes it his business to know these things."

His glib reply told her nothing, but Randy realized that for the moment it was all she was going to get. "How do you plan to contact Morton?"

"We're starting with this letter." Hawk took a folded piece of ordinary typing paper from his shirt pocket. "It will be hand-delivered to his office mailbox tomorrow."

She read the letter. It was a ransom note straight out of a private-eye television series, having the message spelled out with letters cut from a magazine. It informed Morton that Scott was being held for ransom and that he would be contacted soon with the terms of exchange.

"Contacted? By phone?" Randy asked.

"His office telephone."

"The line will be tapped. They'll easily trace the call."

"Calls. Each one a single sentence long. Too brief

to be traced. They'll be originating from several western states."

She arched her brow. "Again, my compliments."

"The other Indian nations sympathize with our dilemma. When I asked for assistance, they readily provided it."

"Have you given any thought to what'll happen if you're caught?"

"None. I won't be."

"You've had brushes with the law before, haven't you? Once I had time to think about it, I remembered where I'd heard your name. I've read about you. You've been stirring up trouble for years."

Hawk came out of his chair slowly and leaned across the table so far that his face was only inches from hers. "And I'll go on stirring up trouble as long as my people are suffering."

"*Your* people? What are you, a chief or something?"

"Yes."

The word sizzled like a drop of water on a hot skillet. It silenced Randy instantly. She stared into his sharp, lean features and realized that she wasn't dealing with a run-of-the-mill hoodlum. Hawk O'Toole was tantamount to a head of state, a holy ruler, an anointed one.

"Then as a chief you've made a grave oversight," she said. "As soon as you mention the Lone Puma Mine, this entire site will be swarming with FBI and state troopers."

"No doubt."

She spread her arms wide and laughed lightly. "So what do you plan to do when they arrive, hide under your beds?"

"We won't be here."

Having said that, he left the table and strode toward the door. He yanked it open with such force, it almost came off its hinges. "We leave in ten minutes."

As soon as the door banged shut behind him, Randy laid her hands on the table and appealed to Ernie and Leta. "You've got to help me. Mr. O'Toole's heart might be in the right place, what he's trying to do is noble and fine, but he's committed a serious crime. A federal crime. He'll go to prison and so will you all." She wet her lips. "But I'll see that you're dealt with fairly if you'll help me get away. Barring that, help me get to a telephone."

Ernie stood up and addressed his young wife. "Leta, is everything ready?"

"Yes."

"Put all the bags you've packed near the door. I'll load them into the truck."

Randy's shoulders slumped with defeat. Not only had they refused to help her escape from Hawk O'Toole, they wouldn't even discuss it.

Four

"Where are we going?"

"Wouldn't you love to know?"

Hawk's sarcasm grated on her temper like coarse steel wool. "Look, I couldn't find my way back to civilization if I had a compass in one hand and a map in the other. The only thing remarkable about this terrain is its monotony. Right now I don't even know which direction we're driving in."

"That's the only reason I didn't blindfold you."

Sighing her exasperation, Randy turned toward the open window of the pickup. A cool wind blew through her hair. A slender and unambitious moon cast pale light on her face. The dark outline of distant mountains marked the horizon, but she could barely distinguish them.

She had soon reasoned why the village near the Lone Puma Mine had been deserted. Everyone else had already moved to the "hiding place." Only those involved in the actual kidnapping and their families had remained at the village. Shortly after Hawk had stormed out of Ernie's mobile home, the caravan departed for a destination still unknown to Randy. Hawk's pickup was bringing up the rear, as it had all afternoon, but he never let too much distance get between them and the van they were following.

"How did you get to be a chief?"

"I'm not the only one. There is a tribal council made up of seven chiefs."

"Did you inherit the position from your father?"

As though he had clenched his teeth, the muscles in his jaw knotted. "My father died in a state hospital for incurable alcoholics. He was only a little older than I am now when he died."

Randy waited out a brief silence, then asked, "His name was really O'Toole?"

"Yes. Avery O'Toole was his great-great-grandfather. He settled in the territory after the Civil War and married an Indian woman."

"So you inherited the position of chief from your mother's family."

"My maternal grandfather was a chief."

"Your mother must be very proud of you."

"She died after giving birth to my stillborn brother." He seemed to enjoy Randy's stunned reaction. "You see, the doctor only visited the reservation once every two weeks. Her labor caught him on an off day. She hemorrhaged and bled to death."

Randy stared at him, compassion stealing over her. No wonder he was callous, having suffered such a tragic childhood. One look at his granite profile, however, and she knew he wouldn't welcome any pity, not even a kind word.

She glanced down at Scott. He was fast asleep, stretched out on the seat between them, his head lying in Randy's lap, his knees tucked against his chest. She wound a strand of his blond hair around her finger.

"No other brothers or sisters?" she asked softly.

"No."

"Has there ever been a Mrs. O'Toole?"

He cut his eyes toward her. "No."

"Why not?"

"If you want to know if I'm getting laid on a regular basis, the answer is that I do all right. But your sex life is much more interesting than mine, so if that's what you want to talk about, let's talk about yours."

"That isn't what I want to talk about."

"Then why all the personal questions?"

"I'm trying to understand why a man who is as smart as you obviously are, would do something so stupid as to kidnap a woman and child off a train full of vacationing sightseers. You're trying to help your people, fine. Your motives are admirable. I can appreciate them. I hope you succeed. But through legal channels."

"That doesn't work."

"And crime does? What good can you do anybody when they lock you up in a federal prison for the rest of your life?"

"They won't."

"They might," she retorted bitterly. "They *should* if you don't let us go."

"Forget it."

"Listen, Mr. O'Toole, hasn't this charade gone on long enough? The men who helped you, Ernie for instance, aren't criminals. They've treated Scott more like a favorite nephew than a hostage. Even you, in your own way, have been kind to him."

She continued to make her sales pitch. "If you let Scott and me out at the nearest town, I'll claim I never knew who our kidnappers were. I'll say that you wore masks the entire time and that for reasons unknown to me you changed your mind and decided to let us go."

"How benevolent of you."

"Please think about it."

His fingers wrapped more tightly around the steering wheel. "The answer is no."

"I swear I won't say anything!"

"What about Scott?"

Randy opened her mouth to speak, but no rebuttal came out.

"Right," Hawk said, correctly reading her mind again. "Even if I trusted you, which I don't, the first time Scott said anything about Hawk, the feds would be crawling all over me."

"They wouldn't be if you didn't already have a criminal record," she fired back.

"My record is clean. I've never been indicted."

"Close."

"Close doesn't count. If close counted, I wouldn't still be hard and you would know what sex with an Indian is like." She drew in a sharp gasp. Taking advantage of her speechlessness, he added, "I don't know which I wanted most last night—to see you humbled, or to see you hot."

"You're repulsive."

His laugh was harsh and dry. "Don't play lily-white with me. Your dirty laundry was aired when your husband divorced you for adultery."

"The writ of divorce reads 'incompatibility.' "

"Maybe officially, but your extramarital affairs were alluded to more than once."

"Do you believe everything you read, Mr. O'Toole?"

"I believe almost nothing I read."

"What makes accounts of my well-publicized divorce the exception?"

His eyes moved over her, taking in her windblown

hair and pristine face, the clothes that were rumpled enough to have been slept in . . . and had been. "I know how easily you're persuaded. Remember last night?"

"I wasn't persuaded."

"Yes, you were. You just weren't willing to admit it."

Cheeks burning, Randy turned her head away to gaze out the window again. She didn't want him to see her embarrassment and know that he'd been right. It disgusted her to recall that, for a mere instant, she had enjoyed his kiss.

She had excused her wayward reaction because it had been so long since she'd felt a man's mouth against hers. Though her mind had denied him, her body hadn't. It had gravitated toward his masculine allure. It had reveled in the scent of his skin and the feel of his hair. The pressure of his hardness against her had sparked a glowing fire in her lower body that, even now, rekindled at the reminder.

She had hoped that her responses were so weak as to go unnoticed. Apparently not. He knew. He gloated over her momentary surrender not only because it fed his insufferable ego, but confirmed the allegations regarding her and her collapsed marriage. Much as she wanted to scream denials, she wouldn't. She hadn't before. She wouldn't now.

She closed her eyes against unpleasant recollections and let her head fall back against the seat. In spite of her mental turmoil, she must have dozed. The next thing she knew, the truck was at a standstill and her door was being opened.

"Get out," Hawk said.

Three things she noticed at once. The temperature was discernibly cooler, the air was thinner, and Scott was lying asleep against Hawk's chest, his arms folded around the man's neck. One of Hawk's hands was supporting Scott's bottom. He was holding the door open for her with the other.

She stepped out of the truck and onto the ground. Rushing water was flowing somewhere nearby. The roaring sound was unmistakable. The hillsides surrounding her were dotted with square patches of light, which, she realized after a moment, were windows belonging to numerous structures. In the stingy moonlight she could make out only a few vague outlines.

"Everyone situated?" Hawk asked Ernie, who silently materialized out of the darkness.

"Yes. Leta's taken Donny to bed. She said to tell you good night. The cabin reserved for Mrs. Price is up there." He pointed out an uneven path that zigzagged up a gradual incline.

Hawk nodded brusquely. "I'll see you first thing in the morning. We'll meet in my cabin."

Ernie turned and headed in the opposite direction. Hawk took the path Ernie had indicated. It came to a dead end in front of a small cabin that, as well as Randy could tell, was constructed of rough logs. Hawk went up the steps to a small porch and gave the door a nudge with the toe of his boot.

"Light the lantern."

"Lantern?" she asked timorously.

Cursing her citified ineptitude, he passed Scott to her. He struck a match and held it to the wick of a kerosene lantern, then adjusted the flame and replaced the glass lamp. It lit up the single-room dwelling, which offered no amenities beyond two narrow cots, two stools, and a square table.

"Don't look so horrified. This is the luxury suite."

Disdainfully, Randy gave Hawk her back and lowered Scott to one of the cots. He murmured sleepily when she removed his shoes and covered him with a hand-woven wool blanket. She bent down and kissed his cheek.

When she turned around and faced Hawk, he gave her a slow once-over. She knew that her fatigue must be evident. She wanted to appear unvanquished in front of him. Unfortunately, defeat was weighing down her proud posture and making her expression involuntarily bleak.

"Guards will be posted outside the cabin all night."

"Where would I run to?" she shouted in frustration.

"Exactly."

She drew herself up and looked at him haughtily. "Will you please give me some privacy, Mr. O'Toole?"

"You're shivering."

"I'm cold."

"Should I send in a young, virile brave to warm your bed?"

Her head dropped forward until her chin was almost resting on her chest. She was too tired and too dispirited to fight with him, even verbally. "Just leave me alone. I'm here. My son and I are at your mercy. What more do you want from me?" She raised her head and looked at him with open appeal.

A muscle in his cheek twitched. "A foolhardy question for a woman to ask a desperate man. I've got little else to lose. It won't really matter whether I treat you kindly or not, will it? I could be hanged in either case."

He seemed to be exercising tremendous control to keep from closing the distance between them. "I despise what you are," he said in a raspy voice. "Fair. Blond. Undiluted Anglo, with all the superiority that goes with it. But every time I look at you, I want you. I'm not sure which of us that discredits most."

With that, he stalked out, leaving her shuddering where she stood.

The sun was just cresting the rim of the nearest mountain. Hawk, standing at the window in his cabin, watched its progressive climb. He was already at the bottom of his third cup of coffee. He drained the tin mug and set it on the crude table beneath the window.

He hadn't slept well.

Years ago he had trained himself not to require much sleep, four or five hours a night at most. He was usually able to lie down and fall asleep instantly in order to maximize those four or five hours. But last night he had lain awake staring into the empty darkness, wishing that he felt better about the situation.

So far, so good. He had nothing to complain about. The abduction had been executed as planned, without a hitch . . . with the exception of including Mrs. Price. He couldn't put a finger on why he didn't feel exultant, why, in fact, he didn't feel good about it at all.

He didn't hear the other man's approach until he was almost on him. Reflexively, Hawk spun around and assumed a fighting crouch.

Ernie took a few steps backward and held up his hands in surrender. "What's wrong with you? You should have heard me coming."

Feeling like a fool, Hawk shrugged off his skittishness and offered Ernie a cup of coffee, which the older man accepted. "It was almost too easy, wasn't it? I keep asking myself what can go wrong," Ernie remarked, while waiting for the scalding coffee to cool.

"Nothing. Nothing can go wrong." Hawk injected

more surety into his voice than he felt. "The letter will be delivered this morning. An hour later Price will get the telephone call from us, followed in quick succession by the others until our terms have been specified."

"I wonder when he'll contact Governor Adams."

"Immediately is my guess. The newspapers will keep us informed."

Ernie chuckled. "They become an asset to us criminals on the lam."

The comment reminded Hawk of what the woman had said the evening before. He picked up a shirt and pulled it on. "Do you feel like a criminal?"

He hadn't meant for Ernie to take his question seriously, but he had. "Not now." He raised his deep-set eyes to his younger friend. "I will if anything happens to the boy. Or to the woman."

The strategic pause coaxed a reaction from Hawk. He suspended stuffing the tail of his shirt into his waistband and gave Ernie a cold, unwavering stare. "What could happen to her?"

"Maybe you should tell me."

Hawk finished tucking in the shirt and buttoned the fly of his soft, faded Levi's. "If she follows my orders, she'll come away unscathed."

Ernie watched Hawk sit down on the edge of the bed to pull on socks and boots. "Leta says Dawn January has her eye on you."

"Dawn January? She's just a kid."

"Eighteen."

"As I said, just a kid."

"Leta was sixteen when I married her."

"So what does that prove? That you're hornier than I am? Congratulations." Ernie didn't crack a smile over Hawk's attempted humor. His taciturn face remained unchanged. Hawk stood up and began rolling his shirtsleeves up his sinewy forearms. "Aaron Turnbow is in love with Dawn. She's just feeling restless and flighty since he returned to college. I figure they'll get engaged when he comes home for the Christmas holiday."

"That gives you four months to enjoy her."

Hawk's body jerked around as though it had been machine-gunned. His eyes were as hard and still as frozen lakes. "I wouldn't do that to Aaron."

"You could."

"But I wouldn't." For several moments the atmosphere was thick with tension between the two friends. Hawk's lips finally relaxed into a near smile. He slipped a knife into the scabbard attached to his belt. "Isn't Leta enough to keep your libido occupied?"

"More than, " Ernie said with a lusty chuckle.

"Then why do you find it necessary to meddle with mine?"

"Because I've seen the way you look at her."

"Who?"

The answer was so glaringly obvious that Ernie didn't even deign to speak the name. Instead, he said, "You need a woman in your bed. Soon. You're itchy. It's making you careless."

"Careless?"

"I could have killed you a few minutes ago. You can't afford to be preoccupied. Especially now."

"When I need a woman, I'll have one," Hawk said testily.

"But not her, Hawk. A woman like her, an Anglo, she would never understand you in a million centuries."

"I don't need you to tell me that."

"Nor do you need me to remind you of the consequences of taking an Anglo woman."

"No. But I see that you're reminding me anyway."

Ernie relented in deference to Hawk's foreboding expression. "Our people depend on you to exercise sound judgment," he said quietly.

Hawk drew himself up to his full height, which put him almost a head taller than Ernie. His proud, square chin jutted out. His voice was as chilling as his eyes. "I would never do anything to jeopardize the welfare of my people. And I have no intention of deserting them to live my life among the Anglos."

They stared each other down. Ernie was the first to look away. "I promised Donny we'd go fishing this morning."

Hawk watched him leave. The furrow between his brows was deeply engraved. That furrow was still there an hour later when he stood beside the cot on which Miranda Price was sleeping, her hands childishly stacked beneath her cheek. Her hair was spread over the pillow in a sexy tangle. Her lips, slightly parted, looked dewy and soft. The sight made his manhood strain uncomfortably against his fly. He cursed himself and his undisciplined body. He cursed her more.

"You should be up."

Having been awakened so abruptly, Randy bolted upright, clutching the blanket to her chest for whatever meager protection it offered. She blinked Hawk into focus. He remained a tall, black silhouette outlined against the sunlight streaming through the window.

"What are you doing here?" She checked the other cot. The rumpled covers had been thrown back, but the bed was empty. "Where's Scott?"

"Fishing with Ernie and Donny."

She flung back the blanket and stood up. "He doesn't know anything about fishing. He wouldn't be able to swim in the swift water I heard last night."

She marched toward the door. Hawk caught her arm. "Ernie's watching him."

"I'd rather watch him myself."

"You'd rather turn him into a mama's boy."

She wrenched her arm free. "He still needs mothering."

"He needs to be with men."

"How dare you advise me on how to rear my son."

"Your son was terrified of getting on a horse."

"He was being carried off by a gun-toting man wearing a mask! What boy his age, or any age, wouldn't be terrified?"

"Donny told me that Scott was scared to death of the goat."

"That's not surprising. He hasn't been around many animals."

"And whose fault is that?"

"I've taken him to the zoo. Not much chance to interact with the lions and tigers."

"Pets?"

"We live in an apartment complex. Pets aren't permitted."

"Something else you should have thought about before taking Scott away from his father."

"His father didn't—" She broke off abruptly.

Hawk bore down on her. "What? His father didn't what?"

"None of your damn business." She rubbed her chilled arms, but, lest he mistake that for weakness, she addressed him with condescension. "I'm very glad to say that Scott is a sensitive child."

"He's a *sissy*. You've made him one."

"What would you have him be? A savage like you?"

Hawk grabbed her upper arms and yanked her against him. She landed hard enough to have the breath knocked out of her and to snap her head back. His breath was hot as it struck her face on each emphasized word. "You haven't seen me savage yet, Mrs. Price. You had better hope you never do." He continued to drill into her astonished eyes before releasing her abruptly. "They've got breakfast waiting for you. Come with me."

"I don't want any breakfast. What I would like is a bath and a change of clothes. Scott needs something warmer, too. We didn't know when we dressed two days ago that we would be kidnapped and carried off into the mountains."

"I can arrange for a change of clothes. In fact, Scott's already wearing his. The bathtub is this way." He turned and opened the door of the cabin. Curious, Randy followed him down the path.

The scenery was spectacular. What darkness had obscured when she arrived the night before, took her breath now. The sky was a vivid blue. The evergreen trees were tall and straight and symmetrical. The ground was rocky, but even the sun-bleached stones added a proper texture to the rugged terrain.

"Where are we?"

"Do I look stupid, Mrs. Price?"

Annoyed, she said, "I just meant to ask if this is part of the reservation."

"Yes. A vacation hideaway of sorts."

"I can see why. It's beautiful country."

"Thanks."

Randy had been right about the stream. As untamed as the rest of the landscape, it tumbled down the mountainside. The sparkling spray that hung in the air like a mist caught the sunlight to create myriad rainbows. The streambed was lined with stones that were as polished as mirrors. The current was so swift, Randy doubted she could keep her footing in it.

She followed Hawk's narrow-hipped, swaggering gait until he stopped a few feet from the stream and gestured with his hand. "Here you are."

She gaped at the crystal, swirling water, then up into the amused face. "You can't be serious. *This* is the bathtub? That water will be frigid."

"Your son didn't seem to mind. In fact, I think he enjoyed it."

"You put . . . you put Scott into that freezing water?"

"Tossed him in naked as a jaybird. As soon as his teeth stopped chattering, he was fine. We almost couldn't coax him out."

"That's not funny, Mr. O'Toole. Scott isn't accustomed to things like this. He could get sick."

"I take it you're declining to bathe?"

"You're damn right I am." She spun on her heels and started back toward the cabin. "I'll wash with the drinking water."

"Suit yourself."

He let her pick her own way back up the path. When she reached the cabin, she slammed the door behind her. She had no way of heating the pail of drinking water that had been left for her and Scott. The cabin had a fireplace, but there was no wood stacked in it. However, the drinking water was warmer than the stream would have been. She washed as best she could with it and was about half done when someone knocked on the door. Wrapping herself in a blanket, she called out, "Come in."

Leta stepped inside. Her smile was sincere, but timid. "Hawk said for me to bring you these clothes."

It was impossible not to smile back at Leta. Her face was broad, her nose short, her lips wide. She wasn't pretty, but her luminous dark eyes and sweet demeanor made up for her lack of beauty. "Thank you, Leta."

She withdrew something from the pocket of her long, shapeless skirt. "I thought you could use this too." She shyly handed Randy a bar of soap.

"Thank you again. I appreciate it." She sniffed at the bar. The fragrance was strong and masculine, unlike the perfumed soap she usually used, but she was grateful for it regardless.

"Here's a hairbrush, too," Leta added hastily, as she handed it to Randy.

Randy turned the items over in her hands. The ordinary grooming utensils seemed precious now. "You've been kind to me, Leta. Thank you."

Basking in Randy's compliment, she turned to go. Only then did Randy take notice of the clothes Leta had laid on the table. The flannel shirt was gray and brown plaid. The long skirt was the drabbest color she'd ever seen. Even military camouflage was more attractive.

"Did Mr. O'Toole choose the clothes himself?"

Leta bobbed her head and ducked out the door, as though she feared Randy might hurl the ugly clothes at her.

Randy finished her sponge bath. She found underclothes folded between the shirt and skirt. The underpants would do, but the bra was several sizes too large. She had already washed out her own. It was still wet, so she had to go without. Not that it mattered. The shirt was as shapeless as the skirt. They hung on her slender figure like a shroud on a flagpole. It was another of Hawk's sneaky methods to try to diminish her will.

She had no mirror, but she did what she could to improve her appearance. She tied the long tail of the shirt into a knot at her waist, rolled the sleeves back to her elbows, and flipped up the collar. There wasn't much she could do about the skirt. She put the hairbrush to good use, however. Once she had worked out all the snags, she used a shoelace out of her sneakers to make a ponytail.

She didn't know what was expected of her, but she wasn't about to sit in the cabin all day. The weather was lovely; it was a gorgeous day. As long as she was being held against her will in the mountains, she might just as well get as much enjoyment as she could out of them. Besides, she was eager to see Scott. She didn't like the idea of him being allowed to roam freely in this wilderness. He was unaware of the dangers.

She stepped out onto the porch and took in the scene spread out around her. There had been few people about when she had left the cabin with Hawk earlier. Now there were many. She would guess a hundred or more. She was also surprised to note the number of dwellings situated on the hillsides. The cabins seemed to be natural extensions of the rock, blending into their backdrops so well as to be almost undetectable.

Hearing Scott's voice over the sound of the rushing water, she set out in that direction. She came up short when she saw him at the water's edge in the company of Ernie and Donny. Standing on his knees and using a flat boulder as his worktable, Scott was using the knife Hawk had given him to disembowel a fish.

"*Scott!*"

He glanced up at her through the bangs that were hanging in his eyes and flashed her his gap-toothed smile. "Mommy! Come see. I caught some fish! Three of them. All by myself. I took 'em off the hook and everything."

He was so excited about his catch that she couldn't scold. She carefully made her way over the stony ground toward him. "That's wonderful, but—"

"Ernie showed me how to bait the hook, and pull 'em outta the water, and work the hook outta their mouths. Donny already knew all that, but he only caught two and I caught *three*."

"Are you warm enough? Did you get in that water? Those rocks are awfully slick. You must be careful, Scott."

He wasn't listening. "First you cut their heads off. Then you split their bellies open. This is their guts. See all this squishy stuff, Mommy? You have to use a knife to get all the guts out so you can cook 'em and eat 'em."

Again, he attacked the fish with a relish that made Randy queasy. His tongue came out to fill the left corner of his lips, a trait that indicated the level of his concentration. "But you gotta be real careful with the knife and not cut your finger off or else it'll get cooked for supper, too. That's what Hawk told me."

"The boy learns well."

Randy whirled around. Hawk had moved up behind her. Though the top of her head barely reached his collarbone, she lit into him, poking his chest with her finger to emphasize each point. "I want you to do whatever is necessary to get us away from here. Call Morton. Get him to agree to your demands. Call Governor Adams himself. Go on the warpath. I don't care how you do it, just get us back home. Is that understood?"

"Don't you like it here, Mommy?"

She faced Scott again. His dirt-streaked face was filled with concern as he gazed up at her. The light in his eyes had dimmed. He was no longer smiling and animated. "I do. It's neat."

"It is not neat, Scott. It's . . . it's . . ." She glanced down at the gore-strewn rock. "It's disgusting. You march up to the cabin right this minute and scrub your face and hands with soap."

Scott's lower lip began to tremble. He lowered his head with embarrassment. His shoulders drooped. Randy rarely scolded him so severely, and never in the presence of other people. But the sight of him having such a wonderful time with his kidnappers, in his innocence not realizing the potential threat they posed, had snapped her control.

Hawk stepped between Scott and her and laid a hand on the boy's shoulder. "You did very well on the fish, Scott."

Scott raised his head and looked up at Hawk dejectedly. "I did?"

"You did such a good job that I have another one for you now. Go with Ernie and Donny. As you know, we brought all our livestock with us. I want you to help groom the horses."

Randy made a sound of protest. Hawk spun around and stymied any others with one fierce stare. "Ernie?"

"Come, Donny, Scott," Ernie said.

Scott hesitated. "Mommy, can I go?"

Hawk's lips barely moved. In a voice only loud enough for her to hear, he said, "I'll separate you from him. You won't know where he is or what he's doing."

She swallowed hard. Her hands balled into fists and she squeezed her eyes shut. She was backed into a corner, just as she had been the first time she heard an ugly and unfounded rumor about herself. She knew when she was defeated and this was one of those times. "Go with Ernie and Donny, darling," she said hoarsely. "Just be extremely careful."

"I will," Scott promised excitedly. "Come on, Donny. I'm not scared of horses anymore." She could hear his happy chatter as the trio made its way down the hill. Then, looking Hawk straight in the eyes, she said, "You hateful sonofabitch."

With one swift and fluid motion, he withdrew the knife from his scabbard and brought it to within an inch of her nose. "Clean the fish."

Five

Incredulous, Randy laughed. "Clean them yourself. Or better yet, go straight to hell." She slapped the knife away from her face. "For your information, Cochise, I'm no squaw."

"Clean the fish or you don't eat."

"Then I won't eat."

"And neither will Scott."

Calling his bluff, she said, "You wouldn't deny a child food, Mr. O'Toole."

Hawk stared at her for a full minute. Randy was beginning to feel smug, thinking she had scored a major victory. Then he said in a low, level voice, "Clean the fish or I'll make good my threat to separate you from your son."

He was no fool and that made him an awesome enemy. If he had plunged the knife between her ribs, he couldn't have found a straighter path to her heart. Knowing where she was most vulnerable, he had appealed to her greatest fear as a mother. Not knowing Scott's whereabouts, especially in this wild country, would be hell on earth.

Shooting him a murderous look, Randy took the knife from him. She studied it for a moment, running her fingers over the smooth ivory handle and the flat edge of the gleaming stainless steel blade.

"Don't even think about stabbing me with it," Hawk told her softly. "They would kill you before I even hit the ground."

When she looked up at him, he hitched his head in the direction of the compound. Several people had noticed them talking together. They appeared to be routinely going about their business, but their eyes were watchful and wary. What Hawk said was true. She wouldn't stand a chance if she resorted to violence. She hadn't considered actually killing him, but she *had* thought about inflicting some damage.

Defeated again, she sank down beside the boulder where Scott's fish lay.

"I don't know how to do this."

"Learn."

She stared at the carcasses with dismay. The smell alone made her want to retch. Loath to touch the fish with her bare hands, she nudged one with the tip of the knife. "What do I do?" she asked helplessly.

"You heard Scott. First you cut off its head."

She finally worked up enough nerve to take the fish that was still intact by the tail. She laid the blade of the knife against its throat. Her first tentative sawing motion caused a crunching sound. With a soft cry, she dropped the fish and shuddered violently.

Muttering swearwords, Hawk reached down grabbed a handful of her shirt, and hauled her to her feet. He retrieved his knife and sheathed it in the scabbard. He called out to one of the Indians. The teenage boy came jogging over. Hawk spoke to him rapidly in their native tongue. The boy looked

at Randy and laughed. Hawk slapped him affectionately on the back.

"Aren't you going to make me do it?" she asked,
as he led her away.

"No."

"There's no need to now, is there? You accom-
plished what you wanted to. You only wanted to
humiliate me. Like putting me in these wretched
clothes?"

"I didn't want you to clean the fish because I
didn't want to waste them. You would only make a
mess of it." He gave her a sidelong glance that mocked
both her ignorance and her futile attempts to make
the horrible wardrobe attractive. "Haven't you ever
cooked fish?"

It was irritating to be put on the defensive. "One
that I bought in the supermarket. I've never had an
occasion to clean one."

"You've never gone fishing?"

She shook her head no. A reflective expression
clouded her face. "My father wasn't much of an
outdoorsman."

"*Wasn't*? He's dead?"

"Yes."

"What happened?"

"Why should you care?"

"I don't. But you seem to."

She remained stubbornly silent for several moments, then said, "He worked himself to death. He
had a heart attack one day at his office and died at
his desk."

"What about your mother?"

"She remarried and lives on the east coast with
her husband." Shaking her head ruefully, she said,
"She married the same kind of man as Dad. I couldn't
believe it."

"What kind of man is that?"

"Demanding. Selfish. A workaholic. No plateau was ever good enough. I couldn't count the number of family vacations that were canceled because something came up and Dad couldn't—or wouldn't—leave town."

"Poor you. No vacations. You had to languish beside your backyard swimming pool instead of the beach."

Randy stopped in her tracks and glared up at him. "How dare you disparage me and my life? What do you know about it?"

He moved his face down close to hers. "Not a damn thing. There weren't any backyard swimming pools where I grew up."

She could have taken issue with him. She could have told him that she would have traded the swimming pool for some attention from her father. He had always been too busy for her and her mother. Whenever they complained about his excessive devotion to work, he defended himself by saying that he was working for them. Randy would then be made to feel ungrateful and guilty.

But with maturity came a deeper understanding. Her father had provided her with material things, but she had been shortchanged nonetheless. He hadn't worked to provide her and her mother with luxuries. He hadn't worked for them at all. He had worked to satisfy a compulsive need within himself.

But she would be damned before she discussed her personal life with Hawk O'Toole. Let him think what he wanted to about her. She didn't care.

It seemed, however, that she was the only one who didn't value his good opinion. As they made their way through the compound, Hawk was stopped to admire a new baby, settle a dispute over a saddle, and assist in hoisting a generator off a flatbed truck.

They came upon a young man who was slouched against a tree sipping from a bottle of whiskey. He nearly jumped out of his skin when he saw Hawk. He hastily recapped the bottle and tossed it to the ground.

"Johnny," Hawk greeted him laconically.

"Hello, Hawk."

"This is Mrs. Price."

"I know who she is."

"You also know why we're here, how important this is to us."

"Yes."

"Just because the mine has been closed doesn't mean we don't have work to do. Let's utilize this time to do some long overdue maintenance work on all the trucks. I'm counting on you to give them thorough tune-ups. Understand?"

Johnny's dark eyes flashed and he swallowed hard. "Yes."

Hawk glanced down at the whiskey bottle. He didn't have to say anything about it. His eyes spoke volumes. "You're the best mechanic I've got. I depend on you. Don't disappoint me."

The young man bobbed his head. "I'll start on it right away."

Hawk gave him a brusque nod and walked away. "How do you know he won't pick up that bottle again?" Randy asked him when they were out of earshot.

"I don't. I hope he won't. Once he picks it up, he has a hard time putting it down."

"Isn't he rather young to have such a drinking problem?"

"He made a serious mistake and he's paying for it."

"What kind of mistake?"

"He married an Anglo." He gave her a hard look. "She hated living on the reservation. Johnny wouldn't leave it because he knew he could never come back. So his wife packed up one day and disappeared. He's been drinking ever since. His ego has taken a brutal beating because he fell for her in the first place, then when he got her, he couldn't keep her."

Randy ignored his sneer and addressed the topic. "You're trying to restore his self-confidence by giving him additional responsibilities."

"Something like that," Hawk replied with a negligent shrug. "Besides, he *is* an excellent mechanic and the trucks *do* need an overhaul."

"You're the tribal psychologist as well as baby-blesser and problem-solver. What other hats do you wear, Mr. O'Toole?"

He stepped up onto the porch of a cabin and swung open the door. "I'm the chief outlaw."

Up till then, Randy hadn't noticed where their walk was taking them. Now, she hesitated on the top step. "What do you mean?"

"Inside."

Hesitantly, she preceded him into the cabin. The dimness was an extreme contrast to the bright sunlight outside, so it took her eyes several seconds to adjust. Several men, whom she recognized as her kidnappers, were loitering around a rickety wooden desk on which sat the first telephone she'd seen since her abduction. Her heart gave a glad lurch, but the somber expressions of the men quelled it immediately.

"Where's Ernie?" one of them asked Hawk.

"He's watching the boy. He said for us to go ahead without him."

"If everything has gone according to schedule, it's time we put our call through."

Apparently Hawk agreed. He sat down in the only chair in the single room and pulled the telephone toward him. He looked at Randy and ordered curtly, "Come here."

"What for?"

His eyes, beneath the black, arching eyebrows, glittered dangerously. "Come here." She shuffled forward, until she was standing at the edge of the desk across from him. He said, "The conversation must be brief. Thirty seconds, forty-five max. When I pass the receiver to you, identify yourself to Price. Tell him that you're safe, that you haven't been mistreated, but that we mean business. Say nothing else. If you do, you'll regret it."

He slipped the knife from the scabbard again and laid it within his reach on the table. "Our honor and our livelihoods are at stake. We're willing to die to protect both and to regain what is rightfully ours for future generations. Do you understand me?"

"Perfectly. But if you think I'm saying a single word into that telephone, you've got another think coming."

Her adamant statement elicited a reaction from the other men. They seemed aghast that she would address Hawk in such a disrespectful fashion. Hawk merely continued to stare at her with eyes that were as steady and blue as a gas flame.

After several moments, he turned his mouth down at the corners and, with a shrug, said, "Fine." Addressing the man nearest the door, he added, "Bring the boy. We'll let him do the talking."

"No!"

Randy's exclamation halted the man before he could

take a single step toward the door. She swapped stubborn stares with Hawk. His stony expression was filled with resolve. He wouldn't relent. That she knew. She wouldn't let Scott be subjected to making the telephone call to his father. That Hawk knew. So it came down to a contest of wills.

Morton was no doubt frantic by now. His anxiety would be transmitted to Scott. There was also the fearsome knife lying on the desk to take into consideration. Subtle as that threat was, Scott was astute enough to pick up on it. What to him amounted to a camping holiday would become the nightmare it was for her. Just as Hawk had counted on, she would prevent that from happening at all costs.

"You win this time," she reluctantly whispered to Hawk. "I'll speak to Morton."

Hawk said nothing. He had been assured of a win before the contest had even begun. Picking up the receiver, he dialed the number he'd memorized beforehand. The line was busy.

Everyone in the room, including Randy, released a pent-up sigh. She ran her sweaty palms over her skirt.

"What does that mean? Did somebody jump the gun, call before they were supposed to?"

"They're all too smart for that," Hawk said. "Remember, we knew when we were going to call, but the authorities didn't. Anybody could be talking to Price."

He dialed again. The call went through. The phone rang three times before it was answered. That would give the FBI time to set up the tracing mechanism, Randy thought. Little good that would do them or her.

The second Morton said a shaky hello, Hawk identified himself as the kidnapper. "I have Mrs. Price and your son Scott." He handed the receiver up to her. Her hands were so slippery with perspiration, she juggled it and almost dropped it before she got it to her ear. Hawk's eyes held her gaze like magnets.

"Morton?"

"Dear Lord, Randy, is that you? I've been so worried. How's Scott?"

"Scott's fine."

"If they've hurt—"

"They haven't." Hawk made a slicing motion across his throat with his index finger. "We've been well treated." Hawk came out of his chair and reached for the receiver. "But do as they say. They mean business."

Hawk yanked the receiver away from her. Everyone in the room heard Morton's muffled voice frantically demanding information before Hawk hung up.

"Within seconds he'll get another call, the first in a series stating our demands," Hawk told the room at large. To Randy he said, "You did very well, Mrs. Price." She watched in silent misery as he held up the telephone wire and cut it in two with his knife. "We won't be needing this anymore."

Now that the connection had been irretrievably severed, Randy thought of a dozen things she might have done or said to give away their location. Any message of that sort would probably have cost her her life, but she could have tried. She rebuked herself as a coward and only excused her cowardice on the grounds that if something happened to her, Scott would be imperiled. She couldn't gamble her own life out of fear for his.

Hawk ordered one of the men to escort her to her cabin and lock her in.

Her despair gave way to anger. "For the entire day?" she shouted.

"For as long as I see fit."

"What will I do in there all day?"

"Fret, I would imagine."

She bristled. "I want Scott with me."

"Scott is otherwise occupied. Since he doesn't pose the threat of escaping that you do, I see no need to keep him cooped up indoors." He hitched his head toward the door. The man he'd directed to go with her grasped her elbow, though not unkindly. Randy angrily worked it free.

"I'll go peaceably." She said it with a sweet smile, but her eyes threw daggers at Hawk. "When they catch you, I hope they lock you up forever."

"They'll do neither."

As she was walking back to her cabin, it bothered Randy that he seemed so sure.

". . . and this was a really big horse, Mommy, not a pony. I got to ride it all by myself. At first Ernie held it on a rope, but then he slapped the horse on the rump—that's what it's called, the rump—and we took off." One of his hands slid off the other in a shooting gesture. "But I had to stay inside the corral. Hawk said maybe tomorrow I could ride out of the corral, but he'd have to wait and see."

"We might not be here tomorrow, Scott. Your dad might come and take us home. Wouldn't you like that?"

His small face scrunched into a perplexed frown as he contemplated that. "Yeah, I guess so, but I don't think I'm ready to go yet. It's fun here."

"You aren't afraid?"

"Of what?"

Of what? she asked herself. Of the evening shadows that seemed longer and darker than they were in the city? Of the purple dusk that came hours earlier when the sun sank below the peaks of the mountains? Of the strange sights and sounds and smells?

"Of Hawk," she said finally.

Scott looked at her, obviously puzzled. "Of Hawk? Why would I be scared of Hawk?"

"He did something bad, Scott. He committed a serious crime when he took us off that train against our will. You know what kidnapping means."

"But Hawk is nice."

"Remember all the talks we've had about never getting into a car with a stranger no matter how nice he or she might seem?"

"Like the yucky people who touch boys and girls in the bad way?" He shook his head positively. "Hawk hasn't touched me in the bad way. Has he touched you in the bad way, Mommy?"

She had to clear her throat before she could speak. "No, but there are other bad things people can do."

"Is Hawk gonna do something bad to us?" His flaxen brows pulled together worriedly.

Too late, she saw that her warnings were doing more harm than good. She didn't want to alarm Scott, but she also didn't want him to make Hawk into his idol. She forced a smile, and, after wetting her fingers with her tongue, smoothed down his stubborn cowlick. "He isn't going to do anything bad. Just remember that he did something that is against the law."

"Okay." He agreed too readily. Her admonition had been the proverbial water on a duck's back and had rolled right off. "Today Hawk taught me how to spear a fish from the bank of a pond where the water is still. He showed me how to sharpen a stick with the knife he gave me. He said it's good to have a weapon, but that it comes with res . . . responpablisity."

"Responsibility."

"Yeah, that. He said you should only use a weapon to get food, or to defend yourself, or . . ." He struggled to remember. "Oh, yeah, or to protect somebody you love."

Randy found it hard to believe that Hawk had ever loved anyone. His parents perhaps? His maternal grandfather who had been a chief before him? The people of his tribe? Certainly them. But a one-to-one love relationship? She couldn't fathom a man as hard-hearted as he loving a woman.

Disturbed over the thought, she said absently, "Always be careful with the knife."

"I will. Hawk gave me lots of safety lessons."

"You and Hawk had quite a lot to talk about. Anything else?"

"Uh-huh. Today when we were tee-teeing in the woods, I asked him if mine would ever be as big as his and he said one day it prob'ly would be. His is *huge*, Mommy. Even bigger than Dad's. Hi, Hawk."

Randy, dumbfounded over the subject of Scott's meandering chatter, whirled around to see the topic of their conversation filling up the narrow doorway. Scott ran toward him. "I was just telling Mommy about—"

"The knife lessons," she interjected quickly. Standing, she faced him, hoping that he hadn't overheard Scott. "I think Scott is too young to be playing with knives."

"He is too young to be 'playing' with them. But every boy, even city-bred Anglos, should learn hunting skills. I'm here to take you to dinner. Ready, Scott?" Keeping his eyes on Randy, he extended his hand to the boy, who eagerly clasped it. They passed through the door together, leaving Randy to bring up the rear.

Scott kept Hawk engaged in conversation until they reached the center of the compound, where there was a buffet line of sorts. The main dish was chili being served out of enormous cauldrons, which had been simmering over the cookfire all day. Each family had contributed a side dish.

People had collected in small clusters around the bonfire. After having their plates filled, Hawk led Randy and Scott to a blanket. He crossed his ankles and lowered himself in one graceful motion. Scott tried to imitate him, almost upsetting his bowl of chili in the process. Hawk held his plate until he was situated as close to the man as he could get without actually sitting in his lap. Randy took a corner of the blanket—as far from Hawk as she could get.

The food was surprisingly good. Either that or she was inordinately hungry. In any case it was warm and filling and helped to ward off the chill in the evening air.

"Everyone's staring at me," Randy remarked to Hawk once they had finished eating. Most everyone was still sitting around the fire. Women were chatting and laughing together. Several men were strumming guitars and picking out tunes.

"It's your hair." The husky timbre of his voice drew her eyes up to Hawk's. "The firelight makes it . . ."

He never completed the sentence. That was disconcerting. So was the exclusively attentive way he was gazing at her. Randy had a sensation of suspension, of falling and being unable to catch herself. She desperately wanted to hear the adjective he had failed to speak, but the intimacy of the moment frightened her.

"I'm cold," she told him. "I want to go back to the cabin now."

He shook his head no.

"Please."

"If you go back, I'll have to send a guard with you." He made a gesture to encompass the circle of people. "They need the relaxation."

"I don't care what they need," she snapped. "I want to go inside."

Holding her hostile stare, Hawk raised his hand. Within seconds a young woman appeared at his side, smiling and eager to do his bidding. He spoke to her tersely. She faded into the darkness, reappearing in under a minute with a blanket folded over her arm. She extended it to Hawk, but he spoke another curt command. The young woman turned toward Randy. No longer smiling, her expression was rebellious and malevolent. She practically threw the blanket at Randy before stalking off.

Randy unfolded the blanket and wrapped it around herself. "What's the matter with her?"

"Nothing." He was frowning sternly as he watched the young woman follow the perimeter of the circle and sit down almost directly across the fire from them. Even from that distance, her antagonism was obvious.

"She's been giving me 'drop dead' looks all night. What have I done to her?"

"She's just high-strung."

Randy didn't buy it. She knew jealousy when she saw it, and the young Indian woman was reeking with it. "Is there any significance attached to my sharing your blanket?"

"Families usually eat together."

"Is that an ancient tribal custom?"

"It is a recent custom that I instigated."

"Any special reason?"

"It's important for the children to recognize the family unit. Father, mother, children. It establishes unity and order."

"So why are Scott and I eating with you?"

"For the time being, you're my responsibility."

"In a roundabout way, your family."

"I suppose you could look at it that way."

"Apparently *she* does. And you needn't ask who. I'm talking about the high-strung girl with the sour expression for me and the cow eyes for you. What's her name?"

"Dawn January."

Through the flickering flames of the bonfire, Randy watched the girl. Dawn had classic native American features—high cheekbones and long eyes that smoldered as hot as the fire each time they lighted on Hawk. They were brimming with lust and passion. Her sensuous mouth and ripely curved figure would have turned any man's head and appealed to his prurient instincts.

"She's jealous of me, isn't she?" Randy said intuitively. "She wants to be sitting beside you, sharing your blanket. Why don't you offer her father a complimentary number of fine horses? I'm sure she could be yours for the asking."

One corner of his lips tilted upward. It was as close to a smile as she'd seen on his austere face. "I saw that same John Wayne movie when I was a kid."

She made an impatient gesture. "You know what I mean."

"Yes, I know what you mean." His smile faded into his usual intense expression. "If I wanted Dawn, even for one night, I wouldn't have to pay anything."

"Ah," she drawled in a way that indicated she was

impressed. "That kind of sexual favor comes with being a chief?"

"No. That kind of sexual favor comes with being Hawk O'Toole."

Properly put down, Randy safely lapsed into silence. She had little doubt that most women would find Hawk desirable. He was an intriguing man. His coldness challenged a woman's instinct to nurture. He was handsome, if one were attracted to the solitary, broody type. His lean, supple body was certainly appealing. Scott's innocent description of his manhood come back to haunt her now and she found herself taking surreptitious glances at his lap. Her cheeks grew warm.

"Something wrong?" he asked, as he stretched out his legs and propped himself up on one elbow.

"No, I just—" Her eyes were instantly drawn to the sizable bulge between his thighs. She hastily averted her head and groped for something to say. "You often refer to children and the future of the tribe. But you aren't fathering any children of your own."

"How do you know?"

Six

"Oh!" she exclaimed softly. "I just assumed . . . I mean you said there was no Mrs. O'Toole."

Amused at her stammering, he snorted a laugh. "There are no illegitimate children either."

She glared at him, furious because he had deliberately baited her. "Then why did you let me make a fool of myself?"

"Because you do it so well."

Randy's temper had been piqued and she was looking for a fight. "If you're so family oriented, why don't you have any children of your own? Wouldn't a few little O'Tooles strengthen the tribe?"

"Possibly."

"Well then?"

"I have enough to do. Why should I take on the additional responsibility?"

"A proper wife would take care of your children for you."

"Do you have any candidates in mind?"

"What about her?"

"Who? Dawn?" he asked, when Randy pointed out

the girl still sitting on a blanket directly across the wide circle. "She's still a virgin."

"I'll bet," Randy said with a snicker. "Are you taking her word for that, or did you find it out for yourself?"

He didn't like her flippancy. Scowling darkly, he said, "I'm too old for her."

"I don't think Dawn realizes that."

"She could easily be my daughter. Anyway, she belongs to someone else."

" 'Belongs'?"

"One of the young men, Aaron Turnbow, has been in love with her since they were children."

"And that matters to you?"

The leaping flames of the camp fire were nothing compared to those in his angry eyes. "Yes. That matters very much to me."

Randy looked away, privately admitting that she deserved the contemptuous look he gave her. She had no grounds on which to insult either him or the girl Dawn. Her only excuse was that she was feeling ornery. And suspicious.

Having lived with her father first and then with Morton Price, she had pegged all men as selfish individuals who took what they wanted when they wanted it. Either Hawk O'Toole was a liar trying to impress her with his nobility, or he was a rarity she had never come across before.

She ruled out the possibility that he was homosexual. But what man would decline the open invitation of the voluptuous Dawn? There just wasn't that much altruism in the world. Randy found it easier to believe that Hawk was lying to her, though why he would remained a puzzle.

The conversation between them lapsed. Both seemed content to let it die. Snuggled within the warmth of the blanket, Randy breathed deeply of the crisp mountain air. It seemed to cleanse her from the inside out.

The ballads being sung softly to the accompaniment of the guitars lulled the listeners. The repetitive rhythms of the songs were entrancing and seductive. Conversations became quieter; some diminished to silence.

The children, Scott among them, who had been playing hide-and-seek in the nearby copse of trees, finally wound down. Scott returned to the blanket and wiggled himself between Hawk and Randy. Wrapping him inside the blanket with her, Randy drew his head to her breasts and sandwiched his cold hands between hers. She kissed the crown of his head, softly nuzzling the thatch of unruly hair.

"Sleepy?"

"No."

She smiled at his telltale yawn.

Couples began gathering their children and stealing away into the darkness beyond the circle of firelight. Randy saw Ernie lean over and whisper something into Leta's ear that caused her to coyly lower her lashes. Ernie shooed Donny toward their cabin. Arm in arm, they followed him.

Hawk had been watching them too. "Horny old coot."

"Is that why he married a woman so much younger than himself?"

A corner of his lips quirked with a smile. "I'm sure lust had something to do with it, but not entirely. Ernie's first wife died soon after Donny was born. He had three other children by her. They're all grown now. Leta was an orphan who needed protection. Ernie was lonesome and needed a wife." He shrugged eloquently. "It worked out well."

Ernie had his head lowered close to Leta's, his arm protectively around her shoulders. Indians were usually depicted as being unemotional and stoic. Randy was surprised at Ernie's open display of affection for his young wife. She commented on it to Hawk.

"One's masculinity isn't measured by how shabbily he treats his woman, but by how well."

"Do you believe that?" Randy was amazed that he would profess such an untraditional doctrine.

"I don't have a woman, so it really doesn't matter what I believe, does it? It's just better for the community if the women aren't made to feel like second-class citizens."

"But weren't the Indian societies terribly chauvinistic?"

"Weren't they all?" With a tilt of her head, she conceded him the point. "Shouldn't societies be improved upon?"

"Definitely," she said. "It just surprises me that you don't hold more with tradition."

He made a noncommittal gesture. "Some traditions should be upheld. But what good is society if half its members feel worthless except to cook and clean and bear children?"

He was a man of contradictions. His mind was complex and his thoughts seemed to take more twists and turns than a mountain road. Randy was too tired to navigate them tonight. Her eyes gravitated toward Ernie and Leta again. She watched until the darkness swallowed them up completely. "They seem to love each other very much."

"She keeps him physically satisfied, and vice-versa, I believe."

"I was referring to a kind of love that transcends the physical level."

"There is no such thing."

Randy gave Hawk a careful look. He had just confirmed her speculations about his personal relationships, especially with women. "You don't believe in love?"

"Do you?"

She recalled Morton's treachery and the emotional hell he had put her through during their divorce proceedings. She answered Hawk honestly. "Idealistically, yes, I believe in it. Realistically, no." She touched Scott's cool, smooth cheek. He was fast asleep against her breasts, breathing damply through his mouth. "I believe in the love between a parent and a child."

Hawk made a scoffing sound. "A child loves his mother because she feeds him. From her breasts first, then from her hand. When he doesn't need her to feed him anymore, he stops loving her."

"Scott loves me," Randy claimed heatedly.

"He still depends on you to provide for him."

"And when the day comes that he no longer needs me, he'll stop loving me?"

"His needs will change. A man child needs milk. A grown man needs sex." He nodded down at the sleeping child. "He'll find a woman who'll give him that, and he'll soothe his conscience for taking it by telling her that he loves her."

Randy stared at him with astonishment. "According to this warped philosophy of yours, what does a woman require after she outgrows her need for mother's milk?"

"Protection. Affection. Kindness. A husband satisfies a woman's nesting instinct. That passes for love. She swaps him the nightly use of her body in exchange for security and children. If the two are lucky, they each consider it an even swap."

"What a callous man you are, Hawk O'Toole," she said, shaking her head in dismay.

"Very." He stood up suddenly. "Let's go."

He caught her by the upper arms and lifted her—blanket, Scott, and all—to her feet. The movement was so sudden, she was knocked off balance. He waited until she regained her equilibrium before releasing her.

Randy was glad that Scott's body acted as a barrier between Hawk and her. The evening had been vividly sensual. The spicy food, the chanting music, the brisk air, the warm blanket, all had enlivened her senses. Their conversation, especially its sexual references, had left her feeling agitated and restless, itchy from the inside out.

She was disturbingly aware of the tall man beside her as they walked through the darkness toward the cabin. Occasionally their hips would bump together. His elbow glanced the side of her breast.

They had almost reached the cabin when a shadow separated itself from the others and stood directly in their path. Hawk's hand stealthily moved to the scabbard at his waist and withdrew his knife.

The shadow moved forward and caught a beam of light from across the compound. Randy's breath eked out in slow relief when she recognized Dawn January. Hawk didn't seem that pleased to see her, however. He addressed her in a harsh tone. She responded argumentatively. He said something more and emphasized it by making an impatient gesture. The girl shot Randy a look that oozed hatred, then whipped around and stalked off into the darkness.

Randy climbed the steps to the porch and entered the cabin. She felt her way across the rough plank floor toward Scott's bed, laid him down, and covered him with a blanket. He'd never slept in his clothes before. Now he was doing it for the third night in a row.

When he was safely tucked in, she returned to the open doorway. Hawk was standing as still as stone, staring into the night. "Did she leave?" Randy asked him.

"Yes."

"What was she doing here?"

"Waiting."

"For what?"

"To see that you got inside."

"I doubt she's concerned for my safety and well-being," Randy said sarcastically. "She probably thinks you're gong to sleep with me."

"She may be right."

Her eyes snapped up to his, uncertain whether he was joking or not. He wasn't. When he turned his head and looked down at her, his sharp features were taut with intensity. He executed a graceful pivot that successfully anchored her against the doorjamb.

"You would have to kill me first," she told him breathlessly.

"No, I wouldn't." He brushed a light, arousing kiss across her lips. "You would trade me the use of your body for your child's safety in a second, Mrs. Price."

"You wouldn't hurt Scott."

"But you're not sure."

She swallowed hard and tried to avert her head. "You'd have to take me by force."

He angled his body forward, suggestively pressing it against hers. "I don't think so. I watched you tonight. There are aspects of our culture that you find extremely stimulating. Right now, your blood is running as hot as mine."

"No."

Her whimpered protest was smothered by his kiss.

His parted lips rubbed against hers until they separated. His agile tongue claimed her mouth with quick, rapid thrusts, then made love to it with slow, delicious strokes.

Breathing rapidly, he lifted his lips off hers and opened them against her throat, drawing the fragile, fair skin against his teeth. "You like sitting on the ground with nothing over your head except the night sky. You like wrapping a blanket around you for warmth."

He kissed his way down her neck and nudged aside the placket of her shirt with his nose. He planted a fervent kiss on the soft, smooth slope of her breast. "You like our music, with its ancient, pagan, provocative beat. You feel its rhythm. Here." His hand came up to cover her breast. He fondled it aggressively, then more gently, lightly grinding her hardening nipple beneath his palm.

Her mind was chanting no, no, no. But when his mouth returned to claim hers, she responded hungrily. Her tongue searched for his. Her hands came up to grasp handfuls of his thick, dark hair. He slid one hand to the small of her back and, applying pressure there, lifted the notch of her thighs against the fly of his jeans.

He groaned. "Why do I want you?"

Randy doubted he was aware that he'd spoken the question aloud. It was one she could ask herself. Why was her body responding to him, when by rights she should feel nothing but revulsion? At what point had desire replaced fear? Why did she want to get closer instead of push him away?

When he rasped out the words, "I want to bury myself inside you," she trembled with arousal, not repugnance. "Damn you," he cursed. "You're my enemy. I hate you. But I want you." He spoke a gutter word, growled an erotic mating sound, and used the hand at the small of her back to secure her against him.

Then in the next heartbeat he shoved her away. He wiped off his mouth with the back of his hand. "How many have been there before me?" he snarled. "How many men have sacrificed their pride and their integrity for a few minutes of sweet forgetfulness between your thighs?"

He backed away from her as though she were something foul. "I won't be so weak, Mrs. Price."

Turning, he launched himself off the porch and down the steps. Randy stumbled into the cabin. She slammed the door shut and leaned back against it. Covering her face with her hands, she hiccuped dry sobs. Her breasts heaved with remnants of passion. At the same time, she was swamped with self-disgust. She quivered with rage against him and his false accusations.

How dare he rebuke her when he didn't know the truth? How dare he kiss her like that?

How dare she respond?

Eventually Randy lowered her hands and stared into the darkness of the cabin, which was relieved only by the meager moonlight coming through the small window.

Of one thing she was absolutely certain. She couldn't wait for Morton to respond to the Indians' demands. It was past time for her to seize the initiative. For Scott's own good, for her own, she had to get them away from Hawk O'Toole.

She had a plan for escaping, but it was so chancy that it barely qualified as a bona fide plan. From every angle, it was riddled with happenstance. So much of it relied on luck. Still, it was all she had. Impatient to act now that her mind was made up, she was going to ignore the risks involved and go with the plan.

It had occurred to her after several hours of floor pacing. She was grateful to whatever muse governed the memory. From out of nowhere, she suddenly remembered seeing the young man Hawk had called Johnny leaving a shed that, she had later discerned, was a garage.

At some point during the evening, she had spotted him slinking out of the building, clutching a whiskey bottle to his chest. As far as she knew, Hawk hadn't noticed him. Instead of joining the others for the evening meal, Johnny had disappeared into the darkness with his bottle.

The young man's dependency on alcohol was tragic. It made her ill to think that she would be exploiting it, but it was the only feasible possibility she had arrived at. It was reasonable to assume that Johnny had been derelict in his duties and had left the keys in at least one of the trucks he'd been working on that day.

If she could make it to the shed undetected, and *if* she discovered a truck with the keys left in the ignition, and *if* it hadn't been disemboweled, and *if* she could get it started, she *might* be able to drive away before anyone discovered she was gone.

There were other considerations. For instance, she didn't know where she was, though she guessed the northwestern part of the state where the terrain was more mountainous. She didn't know how much gas would be in the truck. She had no money because her handbag had been left on the Silverado train. All those considerations could be dealt with as the need arose. First, she had to escape from the compound.

She chose the pre-dawn hour to put her plan into action. Hadn't she read somewhere that the last hour or so before dawn is when normal people are in their deepest sleep? Hawk O'Toole wasn't normal, but she tried not to let that bothersome glitch sway her determination. Besides, she wanted the cover of darkness, but she had to have enough light to see what she was doing and where she was going. She didn't want to use artificial light; she would depend on what was naturally available, which was the gray light just before sunrise.

One of the first obstacles she encountered was waking up Scott. He groaned and burrowed deeper beneath the covers when she tried to shake him awake. She didn't want to alarm him, but every minute that ticked by was precious.

"Scott, please, darling, wake up." She was gently persistent and eventually he sat up, though he was whining and crying. "Shh, shh," she cautioned, patting his back. "I know it's early, but you've got to wake up for Mommy right now. It's very important."

He mumbled another protest and dug his fists into his eyes, which Randy knew must feel gritty. Forcibly maintaining her composure, she knew better than to chastise him. That would probably result in a crying jag. So she appealed to his spirit of adventure.

"We're going to play a game with Hawk," she whispered.

His whining ceased. He straightened from his slumping posture and blinked her into focus. "A game?"

God, forgive me for lying, she prayed. She had never lied to her son, no matter how much the truth had hurt. She could only hope that he would be so glad to return home that he would forgive her.

"Yes, but it's a quiet game. You can't make a single sound. You know that Indians can hear everything."

"Like when they're in the woods, they can hear animals in their caves and bugs crawling under the ground and stuff like that?"

"That's right. So you must be quieter than you've ever been or Hawk will find us and the game will be over."

"Are we playing hide-and-seek? Is Hawk gonna come looking for us?"

"He'll definitely come looking for us." And that was no lie.

She wrapped him in a jacket that had been borrowed from Donny and tied his sneakers. Through the window she tried to locate their guard. She finally made out a hulking shape, wrapped in a blanket, propped against a nearby tree. He had obviously fallen asleep during his watch. So far God was answering her prayers.

"Now, listen, Scott," she told him, crouching down to his level. "We've got to get past the guard first. I'm going to carry you. But you can't say a thing until we're past him. You can't even whisper, okay?" He merely stared back at her, wide-eyed. "Scott, do you understand?"

"You said I couldn't even whisper."

She smiled and hugged him hard. "Good boy."

Gathering him in her arms, she slowly opened the front door. Its hinges creaked noisily. She froze and waited several moments, but there was no sign that she'd given herself away. She stepped out onto the porch. The bulk beneath the tree hadn't moved.

She felt her way down the steps. On the path, she was careful not to lose her balance or to upset a rock. She didn't feel safe until they were a hundred yards from the cabin. Then she broke into a half run, keeping within the shadows as much as possible. A dog barked sharply twice, but she kept on going until she reached the shed.

The darkness inside was stygian. She released her hold on Scott and lowered him to the dirt floor. "Stay here by the door. I'm going to find a truck for us to use."

"I don't like it in here. It smells bad. It's dark and I'm sleepy, Mommy. I'm cold too."

"I know, I know." She stroked his cheek soothingly. "You're such a brave boy. I don't know what I'd do without you to guard the door for me."

"Is that my job? Am I the lookout?"

"That's your job."

He thought it over and said grudgingly, "Okay, but I'd rather play something else. Let's hurry and finish this game."

"It will be finished soon. I promise."

Leaving Scott just inside the doorway and commissioning him not to "leave his post," she went in search of a truck with the keys left in the ignition. She got lucky on the second one she checked. From what she could make of it in the darkness, it was a truck used for hauling. It had high plywood sides attached to the trailer.

She considered scouting around, perhaps finding another that was smaller, more maneuverable, but decided that since time was of the essence and the sky outside was getting lighter by the minute, she'd better use this one.

She went back for Scott and urged him up into the cab of the truck. He went reluctantly. "Do you think Hawk can find us in this truck?"

"That's his part of the game. Our part is to get out of the compound without him seeing us."

Before that, however, she had to turn on the motor and risk waking everyone in the village with the racket. She only hoped that Johnny had worked on this truck before starting his drinking binge. Sending up a prayer and wiping her perspiring palms on her skirt, she reached for the key and gave it a twist.

The noise seemed louder than a rocket launch. The engine whirred in protest. Pressing on the clutch and pumping the accelerator, Randy urged it, "Come on. Please. Come on."

It sparked to life so suddenly that for a moment she stared at the steering wheel in shock. She glanced over at Scott and said, "It started."

"Didn't you want it to, Mommy?"

"Yes, it's just that— Never mind. Let's see if we can leave without waking up anybody."

"Can I invite Donny to play too?"

"No."

"Please."

"Not this time, Scott."

Her harsh tone brought on a pout. She regretted being snippy with him, but she couldn't afford an argument now. She worked the stubborn floor stick into first gear, gave the truck some gas, and gradually let out the clutch. The truck lumbered forward.

Randy almost expected to be met with a wall of Indians armed to the teeth when she passed through the opening of the shed, but there was no movement anywhere in the compound. She gnawed on her lower lip with the effort it required to turn the truck, but she managed to do it. She guided it along, remaining in first gear, toward the entrance of the compound.

She resisted the impulse to thumb her nose at Hawk's cabin when the truck rolled past it. Driving the behemoth required all her physical strength, while her eyes continued to sweep the area beyond the windshield. Chilly as the morning air was, she felt sweat trickling down her sides. Reflexively, her fingers opened and closed around the steering wheel. All her muscles were contracted with nervousness.

There! She could see it. A gate with a cattle guard to keep the livestock from wandering out of the compound. The gate was open. She dared to shift up to second and accelerate. As soon as the truck rumbled over the cattle guard, she shifted into third. The engine protested, but she gave it more gas and it lurched forward.

"How far are we going to go, Mommy, before Hawk starts looking for us?"

"I'm not sure, darling."

She wiped her perspiring forehead with her sleeve. The road was so rough, it was hazardous. The truck jolted over each chuckhole. But Randy felt a relief in her chest, as though a boulder had been lifted off it. "Scott, Scott, we did it!" she cried happily.

"We won the game?"

"I think so, yes. It certainly looks that way."

"Good. Can we go back now?"

Laughing, she reached across the interior of the truck and ruffled his hair. "Not right away."

"But I'm hungry for breakfast."

"You'll have to wait a while longer. The game isn't quite over yet."

She drove for several miles. The road seemed to go on forever. Eventually it had to lead somewhere, she assured herself. According to the rising sun, she was heading east. That was good, wasn't it? She didn't know. For right now her goal was to reach a main highway. Then she would be as good as home.

The sun burst over the peak of the mountain like an explosion in the night, momentarily blinding her.

She lifted her left hand to shield her eyes against it. But when her vision was restored, she was certain her watering eyes were playing tricks on her.

"It's Hawk!" Scott cried, jumping up to stand on his knees. He braced himself against the dashboard and hopped up and down. "He found us. He's smart, Mommy. He's a tracker. I knew he could find us. Hey, Hawk, here we are!"

Randy jerked the steering wheel around. The truck swerved, barely missing the man who sat astride his horse in the middle of the road. Neither the man nor the horse seemed concerned that they'd almost been run down. Neither moved a muscle.

A cloud of dust rose around the truck when Randy brought it to a wheezing halt. Before she could stop him, Scott bolted from his door and ran toward Hawk, who had dismounted. Randy stacked her hands on the steering wheel and defeatedly rested her head on them. She felt her failure from the marrow of her bones to every extremity.

"Get out."

She raised her head. Hawk had hissed the words through the open window. Even as he said them, he yanked open the door, encircled her elbow in a bone-crunching grip, and hauled her down to the ground. Several horsemen had joined them, including the ever-faithful Ernie. Scott was dancing from one foot to the other, crowing his delight over having come so far before being found.

"Mommy said I had to be quieter than I've ever been because Indians can hear everything. And I was the lookout when she got the truck. And then we drove away without waking up anybody. But I knew you'd find us." He spun around and charged back toward Hawk, tackling him around the knees. "Did you like the game, Hawk?"

His frigid eyes moved from Randy's pale face down to her son. "Yes. The game was fun. But I have something even more fun for you to do. How would you like to ride back to the camp on that?" He motioned toward a pony that Ernie had tethered to his saddle horn.

Scott's eyes rounded and his mouth dropped open. "You mean it?" he whispered reverently.

Hawk nodded. "Ernie will hold the reins, but you can sit on the saddle all by yourself."

Before Randy could voice her opinion of the arrangement, Hawk swung Scott up onto the small saddle. He gripped the pommel with white knuckles. His smile was uncertain, but his eyes were bright.

Hawk gave Ernie a terse nod. He and the other horsemen wheeled their mounts around and headed back in the direction of the compound. Keeping off the road, they crested a hill and disappeared.

Hawk's boot heel dug a crater in the earth when he turned on it and faced Randy again. "You made one bitch of a tactical error, Mrs. Price."

She wouldn't be cowed. Her chin went up a notch. "By trying to escape my son's kidnappers?"

"By getting on my bad side."

"Which wasn't too difficult, since you don't have a good side."

"I'm warning you. Tread lightly with me."

"I'm not afraid of you, Hawk O'Toole."

His eyes slowly scored down her body. He said nothing until they met hers again. Then he whispered, "Well, you should be."

Once again, he turned with an economy of motion and swung his right leg over his mount's back. Randy hadn't realized until then that he was riding barebacked. His thighs gripped the horse's sides. She stepped up into the truck.

"What do you think you're doing?" Hawk asked her.

"I thought I'd drive the truck back."

"That's for Johnny to do."

She alighted and faced him, hands on hips. "Then I suppose I'm to ride double with you again?"

He leaned low over the horse's neck. "No. You walk."

Seven

"*Walk?*"

"That's right. Get going." He flexed his knees and the horse started moving forward.

"It's miles back to the compound."

With an arrow-straight arm and index finger, she pointed in that direction. Hawk squinted his eyes as though calculating the distance. "About two and a half from here, I think."

Randy retracted her arm and folded it with the other across her middle. "I won't do it. Short of using physical force, you can't make me take a single step. I'll wait for Johnny to come after the truck, then ride back with him."

"I've told you more than once not to underestimate me." His silky voice carried sinister undertones. "You've already taken advantage of Johnny's misfortune once. Yes, I saw you watching him as he left the shed last night. I figured you'd try something outrageous like this. But would you exploit a misguided kid like Johnny again? What do you have in mind, enticing him with the promise of all the whiskey he can drink before he passes out? No, wait, it would be more your style to grant him sexual favors in exchange for your freedom."

"You're despicable. How dare you talk to me like that?"

"And how dare you take me and my people for brainless fools? Did you actually think you could sneak past me?"

"*You*? That was you asleep under the tree?"

"That was me, but I wasn't asleep. It was all I could do to keep from laughing."

"I didn't know you could."

The barb hit home. His jaw tensed. "I had a good laugh after you drove off. If you hadn't provided me with such an entertaining morning, I'd leave you out here for buzzard bait. Maybe I should anyway. You deserve no better. What kind of mother would deceive her child into thinking that he was playing a game?"

"A mother desperate to get her son away from a criminal, a fanatic, a madman," she shouted up at him.

Unmoved, he hitched his chin toward the camp. "Let's go."

He nudged the horse forward again. Randy stood her ground, her expression stormy. She would have stood there until the elements petrified her if she hadn't thought of Scott. She became frantic every time he was out of her sight. As long as she was with him, she exercised some control over his fate. But when they were separated, she could think of little else but how precarious their situation was.

She sent up a puff of dust when she spun around and started marching in the direction of the compound. She wasn't as careful on the uneven ground as she had been before sunrise. Rocks rolled away beneath her tennis shoes, threatening a sprained ankle. She would have slowed her pace, but she was aware of each strike of the horse's hooves behind her. Hawk's eyes seemed to be boring a hole in the base of her spine. She could feel them there. Like his namesake, he had her in his sights. While she was under such close observation, she wanted to appear undaunted. Pride propelled her forward.

She ignored the blisters she was rubbing on her feet, and the sweat that was collecting around her waist, and the heavy, itchy feel of her hair against her neck. Her breathing became more labored with each step she took. She was accustomed to exercising, but not in this altitude. The thin air began to take its toll.

Her mouth turned as dry as the dust that swirled around her ankles. She was also very hungry. Maintaining the rapid pace soon sapped her reserve of energy. She grew light-headed. She couldn't keep the horizon level. It began to tilt.

She almost stepped on the scaly reptile before she saw it. It uncoiled a snakelike tongue. Randy leaped backward and screamed piercingly. The giant lizard, his bravado spent, scuttled for cover behind a boulder. Hawk's horse snorted. It pranced skittishly, almost trampling Randy. She uttered another sharp cry of fright. The horse reared. She dropped to the ground and barely managed to roll clear before his hooves came crashing down.

"Be still, dammit," Hawk commanded. "And stop screaming." Using his knees, hands, and soothing voice, he managed to get the animal under control. He then maneuvered the horse closer to Randy, who was cowering, her teeth chattering with fright.

Hawk bent down and grabbed a handful of her loose shirt. He used it to pull her up. "Throw your leg over." She was too frightened not to obey him. Her right leg went over the horse's back at the same time she clutched the thick mane with both hands. Her skirt had become bunched up beneath her, leaving a good portion of her thighs exposed to the sun. She tried to tug the hem down at least as far as her knees.

"Leave it."

"But—"

"I said leave it!"

Her breasts rose and fell on a sob. "You won't be satisfied until you humiliate me completely, will you?"

"No. And I'm an expert in humiliation."

"Hawk, please."

"Enough." When she subsided, he placed his lips against her ear and whispered menacingly, "Enjoy the ride. These'll be the last peaceful moments you have for a long time." Then, possessively laying a hand on her bare thigh, he squeezed the horse between his knees and they moved forward again.

"Does it offend you to have my dark Indian hand resting on your white anglo thigh?"

"No more than it offends me to have any creep pawing me."

A facsimile of a laugh broke through his stern lips. "Who do you think you're kidding? Certainly not me. Plenty of creeps have pawed you."

Randy's lips remained stubbornly sealed. She wasn't going to trade insults with him. It was a waste of time and energy. Let him believe what he would. Others had. Many had. She had survived their scorn. She hadn't gone unscathed, but she had survived. She could survive Mr. O'Toole's insults as well.

The horse plodded along. Randy began to think they'd never reach the compound, but her nose picked up the smell of wood smoke and cooking food. Her stomach growled indelicately.

Keeping one hand on her thigh, Hawk slipped the other into the waistband of her skirt and splayed it over her stomach. "Hungry?"

"No."

"You're not only a whore, you're a liar."

"I'm not a whore!"

"You were willing to play whore for me last night."

"I've never willingly played whore."

"No?"

His hand moved down. His fingers grazed the lace panel on the front of her underpants, which she had traded for the borrowed ones as soon as hers had dried. Her reaction to his touch was violently sensual. She felt it deep within her. She gasped audibly. Her thighs, already warm and sensitive from straddling the horse bare-legged, tightened reflexively. Her fingers curled deeper into the horse's luxuriant mane.

Hawk continued to feather his fingers over the lace. An involuntary groan rose out of Randy's throat. "Don't. Please."

He withdrew his hand. If Randy had turned her head and looked into his face, she would have noticed a discernible difference in it. His skin seemed to be stretched across his cheekbones to its absolute limit. His lips were thinly compressed. His eyes looked feverishly bright.

"I'll stop only because I don't want anyone to see me fondling you and mistake my disdain for desire."

The people of his tribe read their leader's mood well and gave the horse and its riders a wide berth. Randy's eyes darted everywhere, but she didn't catch sight of either Scott or Ernie. Hawk guided the horse to his cabin and agilely slid off its smooth back.

"I thought you'd take me back to my cabin," Randy remarked.

"You thought wrong." Reaching up, he again grabbed the front of her shirt and dragged her off the horse. She stumbled along behind him up the stony path. "Is this manhandling necessary?"

"Apparently so."

"I assure you that it's not."

"It wouldn't be if you hadn't tried to run away. If you were going to make the effort, you should have made damn certain you would succeed."

His critically derisive tone pricked her ego. He gave her a shove that sent her reeling through the cabin's door. She broke her fall against the table in the center of the room and spun around to face him, ready to do combat. Her bravery was instantly quelled when she saw him approaching her with his knife drawn.

"Oh, God," she cried. "If you kill me, don't let Scott see my body. Promise me that much, Hawk. Hawk!" She raised pleading hands. "And don't harm my son. He's only a child." Tears spurted from her eyes. "Please don't hurt my baby."

She threw herself against his chest and began beating it with her fists. His knife clattered to the table behind her. Hawk grappled for her hands and finally managed to secure her wrists. He carried them to her back, holding them behind her waist and rendering her unable to move, much less fight.

"What do you take me for?" he asked, angrily biting out each word. "I wouldn't hurt the boy. I never intended to hurt either of you. That wasn't part of the deal. He knew—"

Randy's vanquished head snapped up. Her eyes latched onto his just as her ears had latched onto his words. "*He*?"

Hawk's angry features smoothed out with drastic speed. He reined in every emotion, until his face was an impenetrable mask and his eyes reflected no life.

"*He*?" Randy repeated on a shout. "Who?"

"Never mind."

"Morton?" she gasped softly. "Is my *husband* in on this? Oh, God! Did Morton stage his own son's kidnapping?"

Hawk abruptly let go of her wrists. He picked up his knife again and used it to cut a leather thong in halves. Randy followed each of his jerky movements, eager for some sign that her guess was correct.

The idea would have been preposterous had she not known Morton so well. She knew what made him tick. Since the kidnapping, his name had been appearing in headlines all over the state and beyond. He would like that. He would bask in the free publicity. He would milk it for all it was worth, giving thought to nothing else, not even his own son's welfare.

"Answer me, damn you. Tell me the truth." She gripped Hawk's sleeve. "Am I right? Did Morton put you up to this?"

Again Hawk placed her hands at her waist behind her back and began winding one strip of the leather cord around them. She didn't even struggle. She didn't think to. The probability that Morton was behind this nefarious scheme had erased all other thoughts from her mind. All she could think about was his convincing performance over the telephone. He had poured his heart and soul into his quavering voice, begging to know if Scott was safe. His anxiety had been phony, all for show.

She gazed into Hawk's face, but it revealed nothing. When he had secured her wrists together, he took the second half of the cord and led her to the bed. It had a wooden frame and was stronger and larger than either of the cots she and Scott had been sleeping on. He wound the end of the thong around the railing at the foot of the bed and tied a series of knots that would be impossible for her to untie.

Stepping back, he gave the thong a vicious tug. It didn't give a fraction of an inch. He nodded his head with satisfaction, then headed for the door.

"Wait a minute! Don't you dare leave until you answer me." Hawk came around slowly and pierced Randy with his blue eyes. "Did Morton Price plot this with you?"

"Yes."

Her chest seemed to cave in. She couldn't breathe. Now that she knew it for fact, she wanted to deny it. "Why?" she whispered in disbelief. "*Why?*"

"You'll be brought water periodically," was his nonanswer. "Since you chose to skip breakfast, you can wait for the evening meal to eat."

Only then did Randy fully realize she was tied up and completely helpless. Did knowing about Morton's involvement somehow increase the danger she was in? "You can't leave me here like this. Untie me."

"Not a chance, Mrs. Price. We tried it the other way, you took advantage of my good will."

"Good will! You're holding me hostage," she shouted. "If the tables were turned, wouldn't you have tried to escape?"

"Yes, but I would have succeeded."

Stung, she tried another tack. "I don't want Scott to see me tied to a bed, Mr. O'Toole. It would frighten him."

"That's why he won't be seeing you."

The blood drained from her face. "What do you mean?" she asked, her voice husky with dread.

"He'll be staying with Ernie, Leta, and Donny from now on."

Vehemently, she shook her head. Tears filled her eyes. "No. Please. Don't do that to me." The muscles in his face didn't relax one iota. "If you won't think of me, think of Scott. He'll miss me. He'll want to see me. He'll ask for me."

"When he does, he'll be brought here. You'll be untied during his visits. While he's with you, you won't do or say a damn thing other than what I tell you to do or say."

"Don't be so sure."

"Oh, I'm sure," he replied evenly.

"You've separated me from Scott. What more can you do to punish me?"

"As you've figured out, Price instigated this. Neither of us planned on you being a part of it. Your own foolhardiness is to blame for your involvement."

"So?"

"Scott's safety is guaranteed because he's valuable to Representative Price." His eyes moved over her contemptuously. "But his faithless wife sure as hell isn't."

"He'll never live up to his part of the bargain." She picked idly at the food on the tin plate. Irritated because he didn't acknowledge her remark, she tossed down her fork. The loud rattle caused him to look up at her. "Did you hear what I said?"

"You said that Price won't live up to his part of the bargain."

"Well, doesn't it bother you to know that?"

Hawk laid aside his fork and pushed his plate away. He curled the fingers of both hands around his mug of coffee and propped his elbows on the table as he sipped from it. "I know no such thing. That's what you've told me. I don't necessarily believe it."

"You don't *want* to believe it."

His eyes narrowed. "That's right. Because if Price doesn't uphold his end of the bargain, I've got no reason to keep you around. I'd be forced to . . . eliminate the problem."

"And Scott?" she asked raggedly.

"He would soon forget you. He's adapted to us very well. Children are resilient. Within a year, he'd be more Indian than Anglo." Her shattered features seemed to have no effect on him. He gave a casual wave of his hand. "Of course, he'd be another mouth to feed, another child to clothe and educate, another liability to the tribe. I'd much rather Price made good on his promises."

His matter-of-fact tone of voice instilled fear in her far more than ranting and raving would have. She had to clear the tension and emotion from her throat before she was able to speak. "What did Morton promise you, Chief O'Toole?"

"To bend the ear of the governor. He's going to plead our case with him to reopen the Lone Puma Mine."

"That much I know. In exchange for what?"

"The publicity generated by this fake kidnapping."

"It isn't fake to me," she snapped, thrusting her fists across the table and turning up her wrists so he could see the red welts left there by the leather thong. He took one of her hands and drew it forward for a closer inspection. He lightly stroked the scraped skin with his thumb. Randy snatched both hands out of his reach and shot to her feet.

"Sit down." For all its softness, his words carried a steely threat.

"I'm finished."

"I'm not. Sit down."

"Afraid I'll run away again?" she taunted.

He set his coffee cup aside and turned his gaze on her with the full blast of the intimidating power of those pale eyes of his. "No. I'm afraid you'll stupidly force me to do something I'd rather not have to do."

" 'Eliminate your problem'?"

She had come out of her chair quickly, but he was out of his before she could blink. His hand whipped out and curved around the back of her neck. "Sit down." He applied pressure to her shoulder and her knees buckled. Once she was back in her chair, he returned to his and stared at her across the table.

"Your husband saw a way for both of us to benefit."

"My *ex*-husband."

Hawk shrugged complacently. "I went to him several months ago because I had read in the newspapers that he advocates the Indian cause."

"Because it's expedient and fashionable, not because he's sincerely sympathetic to you. All his convictions revolve around himself. You were misled."

"I laid our case before him. The mine belonged to the tribe." His face darkened and, for a moment, his eyes seemed to be looking into another time and place. Then they cleared and focused on Randy. "It was bad enough when a group of investors bought it out from under us. You can imagine our outrage when we learned it was being closed, with no prospect for reopening."

"Why have they closed it? Is it losing money?"

"Losing?" he spat. "Hell, no. It's making money. That's the problem."

She shook her head with misapprehension. "I don't understand."

"The new owners planned all along to use it as a

tax write-off, nothing more. They don't give a damn that we depend on it for our livelihoods. Selfish bastards," he said beneath his breath. "In years past they've juggled the books to appease the IRS, but they were being investigated on several counts. Initially, they curbed our production quota. Then they decided that in the long run the most profitable thing to do was shut down operation completely."

He left the table and went to the iron stove in the corner. Opening the door, he threw in a few sticks of firewood. There had been a marked drop in the temperature from the night before. But Randy had never experienced anything as cold as Hawk's eyes when he talked about the injustices heaped on the people of his reservation.

"What about the Bureau of Indian Affairs?"

"The BIA looked into it, but the owners have a signed contract and a deed. Legally, if not morally, they own the mine and can do whatever they want to with it."

"So you appealed to the state legislature?"

He nodded. "When I sought out Price, he listened and commiserated. Since I'd had so many other doors slammed in my face, his sympathy in itself was something. He promised to look into it and do what he could." Hawk's tone turned bitter. "His efforts weren't enough, but he promised to look into it further and get back to me." He returned to the table and dropped into the chair. "I was beginning to think he'd forgotten his promise, but a few weeks ago he approached me with this idea."

"Scheme."

"He convinced me that it would work."

"He manipulated you."

"We would both get what we wanted."

"He would. You'd be left with a criminal record."

"The case will never come to trial. He guaranteed that."

"He doesn't wield that kind of power."

"He said he would convince Governor Adams to intervene on our behalf."

"You'll face federal charges. If it comes down to that, I swear to you that Morton won't stick his neck out for you. He will disavow all knowledge of your agreement. It would be your word against his. Who is going to believe an Indian activist with a shady if not criminal record against a state representative? Admit it, your tale would sound outlandish. It would stretch even the most expansive imagination."

"Which side would you take, Mrs. Price?"

"*My* side. Given a choice between the two of you, I don't know who is worse, the manipulator or the guy he buffaloed."

His chair went over backward and crashed to the floor when he bolted out of it. "I was not buffaloed. Price will come through. He knows we've got Scott, but he doesn't know where. He loves his son. If he wants him back, he'll do as he promised."

Randy stood, too, so she wouldn't be looking up at him. "Your first mistake is believing that Morton loves Scott. That's a laugh." She swept back her hair with an impatient swipe of her hand. "If he loved him, would he volunteer him for something like this? Use him as a pawn? Endanger his life? Would you put a son of yours through something like this?"

Hawk's lips narrowed. Randy pressed her point. "Morton Price loves no one but himself. Bank on that, Mr. O'Toole. If he approached you, if this entire fiasco was his idea, then rest assured that he'll make the most of it and then some. He'll get what he wants out of it and leave you holding the bag. You'll be held accountable, not Morton.

"He's running scared about the upcoming election," she continued. "He's afraid he'll be defeated, and justifiably so. This stunt is a desperate measure to win the voters' attention and sympathy. Who could resist a suffering father, anguishing over the unknown fate of his only son, who happens to be, because of the state's unfair custody laws, living with his adulterous mother? He'll remind the public of me and my faithlessness. He's sure to blame my negligence, at least subtly, for letting Scott be kidnapped in the first place." She paused to draw a deep breath. "Did you put a time limit on it?"

"Two weeks. We don't want our children to start school late either."

"Two weeks of having his name in the headlines," she said on a scornful laugh. "Right up Morton's alley. He'll be the lead story on the newscasts every night." She rubbed her forehead, which had begun to pound with a headache. Then she looked at Hawk again. Flattening her palms on the tabletop, she leaned toward him. "Don't you see? He preyed on you worse than the men who closed the Lone Puma. He's using your people for his own gains."

Nervously, she wet her lips and pleaded with him. "Let us go, Hawk. You'll have much more leverage and credibility if you take us back and tell the authorities your story. I'll defend you. I'll testify that you were duped, that Morton put you up to it. When you've been cleared of all charges, we'll see what can be done about reopening the mine. What do you say?"

"You've got a deal. *If*," he added, "you put out for me tonight. Get naked and lie down on your back."

Stunned, she gazed at him in disbelief. "*What?*"

Hawk smiled, though it was more of a sneer. "You should see your face, Mrs. Price. You look like you just swallowed one of those fish you were butchering the other day. Relax. I just wanted to see how far you were willing to go to convince me of your noble intentions."

"Oh, you're a horrible man," she said, shuddering with revulsion. "And a fool. That'll soon become apparent. The newspaper accounts will let us know just how earnestly Morton is pleading your case. You'll see how naive you've been."

Randy made the mistake of laughing in his face. That ignited his temper. In two long strides, he rounded the table and pulled her up against him.

"Don't press your luck, lady. Your husband damn sure doesn't want you back. As far as he's concerned, you're mine to keep and do with as I please." His breath was hot and heavy on her upturned face. He held her head captive between his hands, which were strong enough to crack her skull. "You'd better hope and pray that Price comes across."

"Your threats are so much hot air, Hawk O'Toole. I don't believe you would kill me."

"No," he replied smoothly, "but I would send you back and keep the boy. I would disappear with him. When I got finished with him you wouldn't recognize him. He wouldn't be a sissy city kid any longer, not a clinging mama's boy. He would be meaner than a snake, a fighter, a troublemaker, a pariah of society just like me. And just like I do, he would hate you for all that you are."

"Why do you hate me? Because I'm not Indian? Who's the prejudiced one here?"

"I don't hate you because you're white. I hate you because you, like most whites, have turned a blind eye to us. You conveniently keep us out of your consciences. It's time we got your attention. Taking a blond anglo boy away from his blond anglo mother and making him one of us ought to do it."

She was quaking on the inside, but she kept her chin high and her eyes defiant. "You couldn't disappear. They'd find you."

"Probably. Eventually. But I'd have time, years maybe. That would be long enough for me to convert Scott into a hellion."

Threats on her life didn't faze her. This did. Her courage exhausted, she gripped the front of his shirt. "Please. You can't take Scott away from me. He's . . . he's my son. He's all I've got."

He slid his hands down her shoulders and arms to her hips. He cupped them and pulled her against him insultingly. "You should have thought of that when you were bedding down with all your husband's friends."

Randy gave his chest a furious shove and pushed herself away from him. "I didn't!"

"That's the story going 'round."

"That's all it is, a story."

"You're claiming that all the rumors about your infidelity are untrue?"

"*Yes!*"

The word reverberated in the explosive atmosphere. Then, "Mommy?"

Eight

At the sound of Scott's hesitant voice, Randy whirled around to find him standing in the doorway. Like a shadow, Ernie was behind him. The Indian was looking at Hawk curiously. But Scott was watching his mother, his young face filled with apprehension.

"Darling, hi." Even as she forced a bright smile, she was hoping that Scott hadn't overheard the last few words of her shouting match with Hawk. If he had, she hoped he hadn't understood them.

She dropped to her knees and extended her arms. Scott ran toward her and embraced her tightly. She hugged him back, cherishing his sturdy body, his cold cheeks, the smell of outdoors that clung to his clothes and hair.

Long before she was ready to release him, he ended the hug. "Mommy, guess what," he said, his eyes sparkling. "Ernie took Donny and me hunting today."

"Hunting?" she asked, raking the hair out of his eyes. "With guns?"

"No," he replied, looking slightly crestfallen, "Hawk

said we couldn't use guns yet, but we set snares and caught rabbits in them."

"Did you?" She examined his face with loving attention to detail. Beyond a slightly sunburned nose, he seemed his normal, endearing self.

"Yeah, but we let 'em go. They were little and Ernie said we shouldn't waste 'em."

"I suppose Ernie knows about these things."

"He knows *everything*," Scott exclaimed, beaming a smile up to his new friend. "Almost as much as Hawk. Did you know Hawk is like a prince or a president in the tribe?" He lowered his voice and said confidentially, "He's real important."

Randy didn't want to get into a discussion on Hawk's merits. "What else did you do today? Did you eat a good lunch?"

"Uh-huh, bologna sandwiches," he answered absently, wriggling away when she tried to tuck in his shirttail. "Leta baked cookies. They were real good. Kinda better than yours," he admitted regretfully.

Tears formed in Randy's eyes. "I forgive you for that."

"What'd you do all day? Ernie said Hawk needed you to stay here in his cabin."

"Yes, well, I . . . I was busy all day, too."

"Did you play any more games with him?"

"Games?"

"You know, like we played this morning."

She shot Hawk a dark glance. "No. We didn't play any games."

He leaned forward and whispered to her. "I need to tell you a secret, Mommy."

Randy was instantly alarmed, certain that he was going to reveal that he'd been mistreated in some unspeakable way. "Of course, darling. I don't think Hawk will mind if we move over here for a private conversation." Looking at Hawk, she dared him to object as she drew Scott aside. She crouched in the corner of the one-room cabin and turned Scott to face her so that his back was to the room.

"What is it, Scott? Tell Mommy."

"I don't think Hawk liked our game."

His secret hardly warranted the seriousness of his expression. For a moment she was taken aback. Then, trying to keep her impatience from showing, she asked, "Why do you think that?"

"Because his face looked like this all day." He drew his brows together to fashion a scowl which, under ordinary circumstances, would have been laughable. "And I heard Ernie tell Leta that Hawk was in one of his black moods because of what we did." Scott laid a conciliatory hand on Randy's shoulder, as though their roles had been reversed and he was the wiser. "I know you were having a good time, but I don't think we should play that game with him again, Mommy."

"No. We won't." She didn't have to feign dejection. It distressed her to see how important Hawk's moods were to Scott. He wanted the man's approval. It was obviously important to him.

She drew Scott close to her again, tucking his head beneath her chin and wrapping her arms around him. "I love you, Scott."

"I love you, too, Mommy." However, now that he'd said his piece, his mind was already on something else. He squirmed out of the circle of her arms. "I gotta go now 'cause Donny's waiting for me. We're gonna pop popcorn. He invited me to sleep over at his house. Ernie said you wouldn't care 'cause you'd be staying here with Hawk."

"That's right. But don't worry about that."

"I'm not worried. I think it's neat that you've got a

friend to sleep over with too. Are you gonna sleep in the same bed like the mommies and daddies do on TV?"

"Scott! You know better than that." Her stricken eyes moved to Hawk, who was watching her like a predatory bird from across the room. He couldn't have helped but hear Scott's piping voice, though his expression remained unchanged.

" 'Cause you're not really a mommy and a daddy?"

"That's right."

"Well," he said, tilting his head to one side as he pondered the issue, "it'd probably still be okay if you did. G'night, Mommy." He smacked a careless and obligatory kiss on Randy's cheek and dashed out the door, calling over his shoulder, "G'night, Hawk."

Ernie gave Hawk a steady look. Randy couldn't quite define his oblique expression, but it bordered on being reproachful. He closed the door behind himself, leaving them alone. After a moment of ponderous silence, Hawk said, "Well what's it going to be? The floor? Or my bed?"

"The floor."

His shrug indicated his supreme indifference to her choice. "Come here."

When she stubbornly remained where she was, he frowned, picked up the hateful leather thong, and brought it to her. She winced when he pulled her wrists together behind her back.

"I won't try to escape again. I give you my word."

"Why should I take your word for anything?"

"I wouldn't leave without Scott."

"But you would gain no small satisfaction by slitting my throat while I slept."

He dug into the pocket of her skirt and produced the knife. She had thought she had successfully taken it from Scott while they were hugging. That hadn't been her reason for hugging him so long and so tightly, but when she'd felt the polished ivory handle against her hand, it had seemed like a gift straight from God. She had seized the opportunity to snatch it.

Now Hawk robbed her of it, just as he had robbed her of her pride. "These escape attempts are getting tiresome, Mrs. Price. Why don't you give them up?"

"Why don't you go to hell?"

She brushed past him with as much dignity as one could have with one's hands tied behind her. At the foot of the bed she sat down, where she had spent the entire day except during the evening meal and Scott's visit. Without a word, Hawk knelt in front of her and secured her wrists to the leg of the bed. From a cupboard in the corner of the room, he took down a blanket and a pillow.

He dropped the pillow onto the floor. "Lie down."

Randy wanted to rebel, but she was too weary of fighting him to make the effort. She would conserve her energy and her wits, both of which might do her more good later on. She lay down on her side and rested her head on the pillow. Hawk shook out the blanket and let it drift down over her.

"I'll be back," was all he said before he slipped out the cabin door. He took the lantern with him, leaving her in total darkness. More than an hour passed. Randy wondered where he had gone and what he was doing. Patrolling the camp? Conferring with the other chiefs? Making love to Dawn?

That possibility stayed in her mind. She envisioned them together, two bodies, one taut and sinewy, one soft and voluptuous, moving together—in perfect synchronization. She saw Hawk's face, intense and virile, as his hips pumped against the woman's with supple grace.

She imagined his mouth at her breast, his lips opening and closing around it, his tongue gently teasing against a jutting nipple, his sucking motions fervent and strong when he drew it inside his mouth.

Randy groaned aloud at the longing that rippled through her. She hated her body's susceptibility, but she couldn't deny it. Her fantasy had created a shameless heat within her that demanded to be extinguished. Hawk was the man to do it. He would give his lover as much pleasure as he took. She could tell that by his touch. That morning, his deft caresses had made her ache. They had generated a carnal fever in her breasts and between her thighs.

A picture of his hand riding lightly on her thigh flashed through her mind. She bit her lower lip in an effort to stifle a low moan of desire to feel that hand inside her clothing, against her skin, inquisitive and investigative.

She was so lost in the fantasy that when Hawk shut the door behind himself, Randy started. She pretended to be asleep when he soundlessly approached her and held the lantern directly above her face. She could only hope that the color in her cheeks wasn't apparent and that her breathing had evened out enough to convince him that she was sleeping.

Apparently he was, because he said nothing. He set the lantern on the table and turned it out. She heard the clump of his boots as they hit the floor and the whisper of clothing as it was removed. The bedsprings creaked beneath his weight. She listened for soft snores or steady breathing, which would be her indication that he was asleep, but he outwaited her. While still listening, she fell asleep.

At some point during the night, she stirred and woke up to discover him bending over her. She flinched and stared up at him with alarm. Silvery moonlight coming through the window lined his face and body and lit up his incredibly blue eyes.

"Your teeth are chattering," he murmured in a low voice. He spread something over her. The edge of it touched her cheek. A sheepskin. She had seen many of them around the compound. She burrowed deeply into the instant warmth it provided. Hawk silently returned to his bed.

For a long while afterward, Randy lay there, staring at the window. She had seen the bunching and relaxing of his biceps as he spread the blanket over her. The skin on his chest was as smooth and tight as a drum. His nipples had stood out against it, small and hard. His waist was lean, his stomach flat. Patches of dark body hair had beckoned her eyes downward.

Her breath caught with every recollection of it.

Hawk O'Toole had been wildly, primitively, beautifully naked.

Leta and she were acting as waitresses for the men. They moved from cookstove to table and back again, carrying the heavy enamel coffeepot and refilling cups as they were emptied. The tribal council had met this morning in Hawk's cabin to discuss their strategy. It was the modern equivalent of a powwow.

Perhaps she should have resented them for talking about her as though she weren't there, but she didn't. For one thing, she would rather be informed than ignorant of what course of action they planned to take. For another, she was free to move about the cabin, which enabled her to watch Scott through the window. He was playing outside with Donny.

She could have been invisible for all the attention Hawk paid her. After last night, his disregard was a relief. When she had awakened earlier that morning, the cabin had been empty, but the thongs had been untied and her arms were free. When Hawk came in, Ernie and Leta were with him. It seemed to Randy that he had studiously avoided looking directly at her, just as earnestly as she had avoided looking at him.

During his discussion with the council, he spoke her name frequently, but he had looked at her only once, that being when she sneezed, surprising everyone in the room into momentary silence. As she self-consciously excused herself, her eyes met Hawk's briefly, and she would be hard-pressed to say who had looked away first.

The purpose of the meeting was to await the arrival of the morning newspaper. Someone had been sent into the nearest town, which was still a considerable distance away, to buy a morning edition and bring it back. Finally the errand runner arrived. He shut off his pickup and ran up the path toward the cabin where one of the other men was holding open the door.

He had three copies of the newspaper tucked under his arm and distributed them around the table. His expression was grim. Hawk assessed the messenger's mood before lowering his gaze to the front page, which he read silently.

Randy could see a picture of herself and Scott beneath the headline. There was another picture of Morton, looking haggard. He was playing his role well. Only a truly devious man could carry off a hoax of this magnitude. Only a truly egomaniacal one would have the guts even to try. She was eager to read the accounts. Morton's quotes would make for

interesting reading. She also wanted to know wha
measures were being taken to ransom Scott and
her.

The men around the table began to shift uncom
fortably in their chairs. Ernie raised his head once
and stared hard at Hawk before returning to the
newspaper. One of the men cursed and angrily left
the table to stand at the window. It made Randy
distinctly nervous that he fixed his stare on Scott.

She looked inquiringly toward Hawk. There was
little comfort to be drawn from his expression, which
turned darker with every passing second. He was
grinding his jaw. His hands had formed fists where
they rested on either side of the newspaper. His
brows had formed a steep V over the bridge of his
nose.

"Dammit!"

Randy actually jumped when he banged the table
with his fists and swore violently.

"Maybe there's more in another section of the paper," Ernie ventured bleakly.

"I already checked," the man who had brought in
the papers said. "There's nothing more. Only what
you read there."

"The bastard barely mentioned us."

"When he did, he referred to the kidnapping as 'a
savage, criminal act.' "

"I thought he was supposed to be sympathetic, to
take our side, and plead our case with the governor."

One by one, each man voiced a comment. Only
Hawk remained silent, ominously so. At last he raised
his head and speared Randy with his eyes. Her in-
sides shriveled in fear.

"Clear the room."

Hawk's sibilant words were barely audible.

Everyone glanced around warily, unsure what to

do. The man at the window responded first. He stalked out. The others followed, muttering among themselves. Leta paused on the threshold, uncomfortably waiting for Ernie, who was standing at Hawk's elbow.

"Before you react," he cautioned the younger man, "consider every possible consequence."

"Damn the consequences," Hawk hissed. "I know what I'm doing."

Ernie didn't appear to share that opinion, but he and Leta filed out behind the others. Without having to ask, Randy knew that Hawk hadn't meant to include her in his terse order to clear the room. She remained rooted to the spot on which she stood.

The cabin fell silent. In the background there were familiar sounds—children playing, someone hammering, dogs barking. Horses nickered and snuffled. A contrary engine was gunned to life. But the ordinary noises seemed far away and detached from the thick silence inside the cabin. Except for the fire crackling in the stove and Randy's shallow, rapid breathing, there was no sound.

Finally, when she didn't think she could stand the mounting tension inside her chest a moment longer, Hawk moved. He stood up slowly, scraping his chair away from the table. He came around the end of it and advanced toward her, never relieving her of his stony stare.

When there remained only a few feet between them, he came to a stop. In an expressionless voice, he said, "Take off your shirt."

Nine

She said nothing, did nothing. Only the swift contraction of her pupils and a reflexive shudder indicated that she had heard him.

"Take off your shirt," he repeated.

"No." Her voice was little more than a hoarse croak. Then, shaking her head, she said more adamantly, "No. *No*."

"If you won't . . ."

The razor-sharp blade of his knife made a sinister sound against the leather scabbard when he slid it out. Randy fell back a step. Holding the knife in his right hand, Hawk reached for her with his left. She ducked. He came up with a handful of her hair. He wound it around his fist and pulled up. The pain prevented her from feeling him slice through the flannel shirt from collar to hem, but she sensed the movement of air against her skin. Glancing down, she saw the shirt lying wide open. Shock stifled the scream that filled her throat.

He let go of her hair, but she was too astonished to think of running. He caught one of her hands and, wielding the knife again, made a cut in the pad of her thumb before casually replacing the knife in the scabbard.

Randy gaped at the blood oozing from the wound on her thumb. Speechless and too stunned to move, she didn't even resist when Hawk peeled the shirt off her shoulders. He pushed her listless arms through the sleeves and removed it.

"Your stubbornness will serve our purpose. Having the shirt cut off you will look even better." He squeezed her thumb until the blood flowed freely over her hand and down her wrist. He pressed the shirt against the bleeding cut, mopping up the blood and smearing it on the flannel. "Your blood," he said. "They'll test it." Strands of her hair were wound around his fingers. He carefully removed them and snagged them in the fibers of the cloth. "Your hair." His lip was curled cynically. "They'll know for certain that you're the victim of a savage, criminal act."

"Well, aren't I?"

He looked down at her bared breasts. Randy closed her eyes, swaying slightly with mortification, knowing that he was watching her nipples draw tight.

"Maybe you are." Stepping closer, he took her bleeding hand and drew it to his lower body. He cupped it around his full sex. "I'm heavy with lust for you, Mrs. Price. Should we smear the shirt with a specimen of another kind? One they don't need a microscope to identify."

He pressed her hand hard against him. She cried out sharply and jerked it away. She had cried out in pain, not in protest of his crude suggestion or of the caress he was forcing on her.

"What's the matter?" His voice had changed. It wasn't sugary with menace any longer. The concern behind it was genuine. No longer glittering and sinister, his eyes moved over her searchingly.

"Nothing," she said breathlessly. "Nothing's the matter."

He gripped her arm. "Don't lie to me. What?" He shook her slightly and, when she winced, he immediately relaxed his grip. "Your arm?"

Randy hadn't wanted to demonstrate any weakness, but since he was insisting, she nodded her head. "They're sore from sleeping on the floor in that position. I got cold before you . . . covered me," she finished softly, glancing away. "My muscles got cramped."

He backed away from her. When Randy looked up several moments later, he was still staring down at her. Turning away abruptly, he went to a cabinet and took out a fresh shirt. It was flannel, too, but much larger than the one she'd been wearing. Randy wondered if it was his.

He draped the shirt around her shoulders and guided her arms into the sleeves. The cuffs hung well below her fingertips. While she stood before him like a docile child, he rolled them back to her wrists. That's when he noticed that the cut on her thumb was still bleeding.

Randy's heart almost lurched out of her chest when he lifted her thumb to his lips and sucked on it hard. Their eyes met and locked as he ran his tongue lightly over the shallow cut he'd made. She drew in a staggering little breath that drew his eyes down once more to her breasts. They were covered now by the shirt, but accessible, as the shirt remained unbuttoned. The crests made distinct impressions against the soft cloth. It was sexier, somehow, than her nakedness had been.

His fingertips settled against her exposed throat,

where he discovered the slight discoloration his strong kiss two nights before had left. He rubbed the mark tenderly. Randy saw regret, and an unmistakable trace of pride, in his eyes.

His fingers trailed down and edged aside the flannel to reveal one of her breasts. It looked pale and pink and fragile against the masculine material of the shirt and his bronze hand. He stroked the inside curve of it with his knuckle. His thumb fanned the delicate nipple until the texture changed and it no longer looked innocent, but erotic. His eyes swept up to hers. Hers were filled with wonder over this soft, caring side of Hawk O'Toole. His were hot with desire.

Then, as if angry with her, or with himself, he yanked his hand back and turned away. For a long moment he stood in the center of the room, his whole body taut and rigid. When he spoke, his voice was gruff. "It appears that your husband doesn't care if you are returned or not."

"I told you he wouldn't." She was having difficulty speaking. Her knees seemed to have liquefied. The lower part of her body was throbbing and moist with want. The heat of shame burned in her cheeks. Quietly she added, "And he's not my husband."

"He's still concerned for Scott."

"Because that's what the public expects him to be."

"He says little about us, about our cause, to the press." He spun around and shook the blood-stained shirt at her. "That's what this is for. To remind him of the terms of our agreement."

"I doubt it'll do any good. He might not even publicly acknowledge that he's received it."

"I'm not sending it to him. I'm mailing it directly to Governor Adams, along with a letter detailing what we want and why the Lone Puma Mine is so important to the economy of the reservation."

"On that score, Hawk, I hope you get what you want. I sincerely do. But you must take Scott and me back. Sending bloody clothes through the mail, issuing silent threats of violence, that's dangerous and stupid. It'll hurt you far more than it will help."

"I didn't ask for your advice. I don't need it." His eyes moved down to the open shirt where the twin crescents of her breasts came together to form a soft valley. "I can think of only one field you might be an expert in," he said sardonically, "and I already know how to do it."

Leaving her aghast with rage, he stamped out and slammed the door.

"He hasn't had an easy life. That's why he seems so hard sometimes," Leta told Randy solemnly. "Underneath, I think Hawk is softhearted. He just doesn't want anyone to know it because that would make him look weak. He takes his job as a tribal leader very seriously."

Randy could only agree. They were at the table in Hawk's cabin, chopping up vegetables to go into a stew. Randy hadn't seen Hawk since he had slammed the door behind himself several hours earlier, taking the blood-stained shirt with him. She had been somewhat surprised that he had neglected to tie her up before he left, but that was explained a few minutes later when Leta arrived. She had brought some mending and a basket of vegetables with her—along with a Band-Aid for the cut on Randy's thumb.

"You're my watchdog, I guess," Randy had remarked. When Leta's guileless smile collapsed, Randy regretted the unkind words. It wasn't the girl's fault that she was the captive of a man without a human heart. Leta was only obeying the directives of a man, a chief, which she had probably been conditioned to do since she could understand the language. "I'm sorry I was so cross with you, Leta. There's coffee left. Would you like some?"

It seemed ludicrous to play house when the lord of the manor had cut a shirt away from her body, assaulted her with a knife, and insulted her in the most demeaning way. Leta, however, had seemed unaware of the inconsistencies of the situation and gladly accepted the cup of coffee. She had started on her mending and when that was finished, began chopping the vegetables, chatting all the while.

Randy had been glad that the conversation had gradually and naturally turned to Hawk O'Toole. She had wanted to learn all she could about him without having to ask direct questions. As it turned out, there was no need to. Leta happily supplied her with uncensored information.

"I haven't seen much of his softheartedness," Randy said now, dunking one peeled potato into the basin of cold water and reaching for another.

"Oh, it's there. He still mourns his mother and the brother who died at birth. He misses his grandfather."

"From what I understand, he must have been the only positive and stable influence in Hawk's life."

Leta digested that, then agreed with a nod. "Hawk and his father fought like cats and dogs. Hawk didn't shed a single tear when he died. I'm too young to remember, but Ernie told me." She counted the carrots she had peeled and chopped and decided to add one more to the basin. "Ernie's oldest son and Hawk are the same age. They played football together in college."

"College?"

"Hmm. They both got degrees in engineering. Dennis does something with dams and bridges. Hawk returned to the reservation when his grandfather died. He gave up a career in the city."

Randy forgot about the half-peeled potato in her hand. "If he left a promising career in the city, he must have felt a strong compulsion to come back."

"I think it was because of his father and the mine."

"His father and the mine?"

"I don't know everything about it, but Hawk's father was the mine manager. He wasn't"—she lowered her voice—"he wasn't very reliable. Ernie says he was drunk most of the time. Anyway, he let these men talk him into selling them the mine."

Randy tried not to appear eager to hear more, but she wet her lips expectantly. "*He* sold the mine to the group of investors?"

"Yes. I've heard Ernie say the tribe was swindled. Most everybody blamed Hawk's father. He finally got crazy with liquor and had to be taken away."

"So Hawk assumed his responsibilities, along with the blame," Randy quietly finished the story for herself.

That explained a lot about Hawk O'Toole. He not only wanted to keep the mine operational for the tribe's livelihood, he wanted to get it back in order to redeem himself. With his college degree and leadership qualities, he could work mines anywhere in the world, but he stayed on the reservation, not only because he was an appointed chief, but because he was shackled to it by guilt.

"Ernie worries about Hawk," Leta went on, unaware of Randy's private musings. "He thinks Hawk should get married and have children. Then maybe he wouldn't get in his black moods so often. Ernie says Hawk is lonely. That's what makes him act mean sometimes. He could choose any unmarried woman in the tribe he wanted for his wife, but he hasn't."

"Does he ever choose one to . . . you know, to . . ."

Leta's eyes lowered demurely. "When he wants a woman that way, he goes to the city for a few days."

Randy swallowed with difficulty. "How often does he go into the city?"

"It varies," Leta said with a shrug. "Several times a month."

"I see."

"Sometimes he stays for days. But those are the times when he comes back the grumpiest. It's like the longer he's with a bought woman, the less he likes it." She wiped her hands on a cup towel and gathered the peelings into the newspaper that had been spread out on the table for that purpose.

"Prostitutes won't get him children either."

"He's told Ernie that he'll never have any."

"Oh? Why?"

"Ernie thinks he's afraid to because of his mother. He watched her die." Most of Randy's antagonism collapsed upon itself. It was difficult to carry grudges against someone who had suffered such untold sorrow.

"If Hawk doesn't start having children soon," Leta said on a lighter note, "he'll have to work doubly hard to catch up to Ernie." She gave Randy a shy, secretive smile.

"You're pregnant?" Leta's eyes danced as she bobbed her head up and down. "Have you told Ernie?"

"Just last night."

"Congratulations to you both."

Leta giggled. "Ernie's got grandchildren already, but he's as proud as a peacock about the baby."

Glancing down at her stomach, she affectionately smoothed her hand over it.

Her soft, loving expression made her plain face beautiful. Randy was glad for her, but she also felt a pang of jealousy. Leta's love for Ernie was so uncomplicated, their lives simple. Of course, he had committed a felony and might very well go to prison for it, but for nothing in the world would she have mentioned that to Leta and clouded the young woman's happiness.

A few minutes later, Donny and Scott came charging in. They stuffed down a lunch of sandwiches, which Leta and Randy made for them. Randy sat close to Scott, touching him at every opportunity without making it obvious and embarrassing for him.

"Gee, Mommy, sleeping over at Donny's house was fun! Ernie told us ghost stories, *Indian* ghost stories." He gulped his milk and wiped his mouth on the back of his hand. "Did you have a good time sleeping over at Hawk's house?"

Her smile faltered. "It was okay."

"Hawk said he would take us horseback riding after lunch. And he said for you to make him a sandwich. I'm s'posed to bring it to him."

She wanted to send back a message that Mr. O'Toole could damn well return to the cabin and make his own sandwich, but she didn't want to involve Scott in their quarrel, as, no doubt, Hawk had counted on. After handing Scott two wrapped sandwiches, she hugged him close. "Be careful. Remember you're a new rider. Don't take any unnecessary risks."

"I won't. Besides, Hawk'll be there. Wait, Donny! I'm coming."

He raced out the door, across the porch, and down

the steps without giving her a backward glance. When she turned around, Leta was looking at her sympathetically.

"Hawk won't let anything bad happen to Scott. I know he won't."

Randy smiled feebly. "He won't as long as I cooperate. Which I intend to do." She took a deep breath. "So there's no reason for you to stay here with me. I know you must have other chores to attend to. Please go on with your business. I'm not going anywhere."

"You tried to run away."

"I won't try that again."

"You should have known Hawk would find you."

"I guess I did. But I had to try."

Leta, unable to understand Randy's determination, shook her head. "I'd rather have a man's protection than be alone."

The candid observation disturbed Randy. Why did being under Hawk's protection suddenly sound so appealing? She wanted to be by herself to think about that. Too, the rough night she had spent was now being felt. Her eyes were sandy from lack of sleep. She couldn't contain her yawns and had given up trying to politely hide them. She urged Leta to leave her alone. Eventually the younger woman capitulated.

As soon as the door closed behind Leta, Randy staggered to the bed. She lay down, pulled the blanket over herself, and buried her head in the pillow. If Hawk didn't like her taking a nap in his bed, that was just too damn bad. It was his fault she hadn't gotten much sleep. First he had forced her to lie on the hard floor. Then he had almost let her freeze to death before covering her up. Then he had appeared in front of her naked.

On that delicious memory she sank into a deep sleep.

He was in the cabin with her when she woke up. She eased herself into a sitting position, shivering with a slight chill, and glanced around the room. Hawk was sitting near the stove, unmoving, slouched in a straight-back chair. His booted feet were stretched far out in front of him, his hands loosely clasped over his belt buckle. His eyes were unblinkingly on her. She got the impression that they had been for some time.

"I'm sorry," Randy said nervously, throwing off the blanket and swinging her feet to the floor. "What time is it?"

"What difference does it make?"

"None, I guess. I didn't intend to sleep so long." Checking the degree of light in the window, she could tell that it was late afternoon. The sun had already slipped behind the mountains. Shadows beyond the cabin walls were growing long and dark.

"Aren't you curious?"

She rubbed her hands up and down her arms to ward off the chill. "About what?"

"About the shirt."

"Did you mail it?"

"Yes."

"I'm all for that, if it'll get us home sooner." She stood up and smoothed down the helplessly wrinkled skirt, which had been dreadfully ugly to begin with. "Did you take Scott horseback riding?"

"He did very well."

"Where is he?"

"I believe they're playing a card game in Ernie's cabin."

"I guess I'll see him at dinner."

"You missed dinner. We ate early this evening."

"You mean I won't be able to see Scott until to-morrow? Why didn't you wake me up?" she asked angrily.

He ignored both her anger and her question and asked one of his own. "Why do you keep rubbing your arms?"

"Because I'm cold. I don't feel well." To her mortifi-cation, tears began collecting in her eyes. "My head is stuffy. I ache all over, and it's your fault. I could use an aspirin. The cut on my thumb catches on everything and keeps reopening."

"I sent you a Band-Aid."

"It came off while I was washing *your* dishes!" she shouted. "I want to see my son. I want to kiss him good night. You've kept him away from me most of the day."

He rolled off his spine and came to his feet. "You should have thought of that before you attempted to escape."

"How long will you go on punishing me?"

"Until I'm convinced you've learned your lesson."

Her head dropped forward in defeat. A tear rolled down her cheek. "Please, Hawk. Let me see Scott. Just for five minutes."

He placed his finger beneath her chin and jerked it up. He studied her face for several moments, then released her suddenly. He gathered the blanket off the bed and took another folded one from a shelf. "Come on," he said, heading for the door.

She followed him gladly, wiping the tears off her cheeks as she trotted after him down the path. She thought it odd that he headed straight for his pickup, but supposed that they were going to drive instead of walk to the other cabin. However, when he struck off in the opposite direction, she turned to him.

"What are you doing? Where are you taking me?"

"You'll find out soon enough. Just enjoy the ride. It's a beautiful night."

"I want to see Scott."

He said nothing, but continued to stare stonily through the windshield. Randy wasn't going to give him the satisfaction of seeing her cry again. She refused to beg. So she squared her body with the dashboard and continued to stare straight ahead, keeping her back rigid and her chin high. She could kick herself for crying and pleading. Not only had it humbled her, it hadn't done any good.

They didn't go far, but when Hawk brought the pickup to a stop, the surrounding landscape was considerably more primitive than the compound. Randy glanced at him with dismay when he cut the motor and pushed in the emergency brake pedal.

"Where are we? What are we doing here? Is this where you're going to bury my body?"

Saying nothing, Hawk got out on his side and came around for her. She stepped to the ground and waited until he took the blankets out of the pickup's bed.

"Up there," he said.

Warily, she preceded him up the incline. When they crested it she paused to catch her breath, not only because of the steep climb but because the scenery was breathtaking in the most literal sense. It seemed that the entire world was spread out beneath them and that nothing stood between them and the sunset.

Its hues were vivid, from the most flaming vermilion to the most iridescent violet. With each second of deepening darkness, stars were popping out like new flowers after a spring rain. Just above the horizon, the half-moon was large and as unblemished as fine china. A cool wind molded her clothes to her body.

"We have to squeeze through there," Hawk said close to her ear.

"Through where?" It seemed that he was pointing to a wall of solid stone.

"Here." Taking her hand, he drew her forward.

Upon closer inspection she noticed a crevice in the rock, barely wide enough to accommodate a slender person. Hawk nudged her forward and she squeezed herself through. He followed. The passage widened marginally at the other end. When Randy stepped through, she was brought up short.

Only a few feet in front of her was a small pool of water. Steam rose out of it like a boiling cauldron, covering the ground with a swirling mist that curled around her ankles and calves. Underground springs caused the water to bubble.

"Welcome," Hawk said, "to Mother Nature's version of a hot tub."

Ten

The prospect of submerging herself in the churning
hot water was a delightful one. It had been several
days since she had had a real bath. She hadn't
wanted to bathe in the frigid waters of the stream,
so, since her kidnapping, she'd had to make do with
sponge baths out of a washbowl.

"Would you like to get in?" Hawk asked.

"Yes," she cried excitedly. Then, with more composure, she added, "If it's all right."

"That's why I brought you here. Maybe the hot
water will clear your head and soak the chill out of
your bones."

She took a step toward the pool before she realized that she was fully dressed. "What about my
clothes?"

"Take them off."

"I don't want to."

"Then they'll get wet."

He began unbuttoning his shirt. When he arched
back his shoulders and pulled the shirttail from his
waistband, Randy averted her eyes, knowing full

well he was trying to intimidate her. She wasn't going to let him. Belligerently, she worked off her sneakers and peeled off her socks, carefully laying them on a dry, flat rock. She unfastened the skirt and let it fall around her feet, then stepped out of it. The oversized shirt reached the middle of her thighs, covering her adequately.

Hearing the rasp of Hawk's zipper over the gurgling of the water, she moved forward as swiftly as the stony ground would permit, and stepped into the pond. She yelped softly. The water felt scalding on her cold feet, but she forced herself to step into it. After a few seconds she became accustomed to it and eased herself down until the water bubbled around her waist, then her shoulders. Finally she was neck-deep in heavenly sensation.

A man-made hot tub would have to have a thousand jets installed to compare to this one, she thought. From every direction water gushed toward her, massaging the soreness out of her muscles, lubricating her stiff joints, and warming her chilled skin.

"How do you like it?"

She was afraid to turn her head and look at him, but she chanced it and was relieved to find that he, too, was submerged up to his chin in the water. Below the roiling surface, she knew he was naked. She tried not to think about it. "It's wonderful. How'd you find it?"

"My grandfather used to treat me to this after a day of hunting. Then when I got older, I'd bring girls here."

"I don't think I need to ask what for."

He actually grinned. "The water has a way of melting inhibitions. After a few minutes of it girls forgot how to say no."

"Were there a lot of them?"

"Girls?" he asked with a shrug. "Who was counting? They came and went."

"In adequate numbers?"

His laugh was low and self-derisive. "To a young man, is any number of women adequate?"

"And now that you're older?"

He watched her closely. "Is any number of women adequate?"

Knowing it would be prudent not to pursue the discussion, she plunged on anyway. "Leta told me about your trips into the city. Do hired women satisfy you?"

"Yes. And I satisfy them too." Randy glanced away. "What about you?" he asked smoothly. "Are you ever satisfied? How many lovers does it take to put out your fire?"

She ground her teeth in an effort to hold in a scathing comeback. Instead she said, "You think I'm a slut. I think you're a criminal. Each of us thinks the other deserves to be punished. Fine. Can't we leave it at that and stop insulting each other? Especially now. Let's not argue and spoil this. Please. It feels too lovely. I don't want to ruin it by engaging in a silly argument."

He turned his head away. His profile formed a dark silhouette against the western horizon, which was quickly losing its battle with the night. Randy appreciated his profile for its masculine beauty.

How would she have felt about Hawk O'Toole if she had met him at another time and in another place, she wondered. If she hadn't married Morton Price so young to escape an unhappy household, she might have met a man like Hawk, strong but unselfish, working for causes instead of dollars, a leader without personal ambition. She might have fallen hopelessly in love with him.

Shaking her head to clear it of such ludicrous notions, she said, "Tell me about your grandfather."

"What about him?"

"Did you love him?"

His head came back around quickly, suspiciously. When he saw that she wasn't ridiculing him, he answered, "I respected him."

She encouraged him to talk, and soon he was relating stories about his childhood and youth. He even smiled at some of his fondest recollections. As he concluded a particularly amusing anecdote, however, his smile inverted itself into a frown.

"But the older I got, the more I realized that I had two strikes against me."

"What?"

"Being an Indian and having a drunk for a father. If folks weren't put off by one, they sure as hell were by the other."

She weighed the advisability of opening up a can of worms, but decided that she had nothing to lose and a lot to gain if she could understand him better. "Hawk," she began tentatively, "Leta told me about your father, about his losing the mine to the swindlers."

"Dammit." He sat up straight so that the waterline came to just below his waist. It sluiced down his smooth chest. Droplets got caught in the dark hair whorling around his navel. Randy wanted to stare at that intriguing spot, but his angry eyes drew her attention. "What else did Leta blab to you about?"

"It wasn't her fault," Randy said quickly. She didn't want the young woman to get into trouble for divulging tribal secrets. "I asked her about you."

"Why?"

She looked at him, puzzled. "Why?"

"Yes, why? Why were you so curious about me?"

"I thought that maybe if I knew more about your background, I would understand your motivations. And I do," she stressed. "Now I know why it's so important to you to regain ownership of the mine. You want to make up for your father's downfall." She laid a hand on his arm. "Hawk, no one blames you. It's not your fault that—"

He shook off her hand and stood up. "The last thing I want from you is pity. If anything, Mrs. Price, you should be begging for mine."

He turned and was about to step out of the pool when Randy reached up and caught his hand. She used it to lever herself out of the water and at the same time to launch a verbal attack. "I don't pity you, you mule-headed jerk! I was only trying to get inside your head, to understand you."

He grabbed her by the shoulders, lifting her up so that only the tips of her toes touched the bottom of the pool. "You could never understand me because your skin isn't tinted. You haven't been laughed at by bigots or fawned over by phony bleeding hearts. You've never had to prove your worthiness as a human being every day of your life. Your successes weren't measured *in spite of* or your failures *because of*. You won acceptance by society the day you were born. I'm still struggling to earn it."

She threw off his grasping hands. "Doesn't that chip on your shoulder get awfully heavy? Don't you ever want to sling it off and be rid of it? No one is as prickly about your heritage as you are," she cried, poking his chest with her index finger. "Nobody burdens you with your father's failings except *you*. You make things difficult for yourself because you feel you deserve the punishment for what he did. That's stupid. Crazy."

His features had evened out to convey indifference, but his eyes gave him away. They were turbulent, seething with rage. "You forget your place."

"My place!" she shrieked. "And just what might my *place* be?"

"Beneath a man," he growled, pulling her against him. He lowered his head and kissed her hard. She squirmed against him, trying to get away, but he was indisputably in control. His tongue continued to probe her lips until they separated, then it masterfully sank into the wet heat of her mouth. He used it to stroke and to tease, to wear down her resistance. It worked. Randy's struggles to be released became efforts to get closer.

She participated in the kiss, welcoming the wicked thrusts of his tongue. But she wasn't ready for the gentle suction he applied, drawing her tongue inside his mouth. Once the electrifying shock had worn off, she explored it with rampant curiosity and carnal delight.

Her bare thighs pressed against his. The hard muscles of his chest rippled against her breasts each time he moved his arms to hold her tighter. She groaned audibly when she felt the steely evidence of his desire against her belly.

Hawk set her away from him. Their eyes locked and held for several moments while they regained their breath. The wind cooled their feverish bodies and the mountain air cleared their heads. The water bubbled around their legs. But nothing served to dissipate their passionate desire for each other.

His gaze dropped to her breasts and Randy heard him take a sharp, quick breath. Her nipples were tenting the wet fabric that clung to her body. Hawk reached for the top button of her shirt. Hypnotized by his eyes, she let him undo it. Then the second button. His knuckles bumped into her breasts and grazed her stomach as they moved down from one button to the next.

Finally all the buttons were undone and he pushed the clinging cloth aside. His eyes roamed over her for a long time, thirstily taking in the smooth, pale globes of her breasts and their dark, raised centers.

Making a low, hungry sound, he slipped his hands inside the shirt and beneath her arms so that her breasts fit into the notches between his thumbs and fingers. He tested their sensitivity by stroking the dusky tips. They responded. Quickly ducking his head, he took one into his hot, tugging mouth.

Reflexively, Randy's back arched. Her head fell back. Her hips slammed into his hardness. He raised his head and uttered a stream of blue words, sexual words, that shamefully thrilled her. Taking her hand, he dragged her with him out of the pool. Together they lay down on one of the blankets.

"Add another crime to my credit," he told her as he peeled off her underpants. He bent over her, kissed her belly, kissed her breasts, kissed her mouth again and again. The velvety tip of his sex was already pearled with moisture when he entered her. He stretched into her, reaching, stroking, unable to get high enough.

Randy gasped with the shock of his total possession. As he moved within her, the glorious sky seemed to open above her. She closed her eyes against the incandescent light, but it continued to shower her with sparks. Her body felt infused with a heat as intense as each burning star. She began to tremble. Only then did Hawk bury his face in her hair and surrender to an explosion of release.

Lying entwined between the blankets, she turned

her face into his chest. She kissed it shyly and caressed the smooth, supple skin with her fingertips. "I'm just another of the girls whose inhibitions melted in the pool."

"No." He rolled toward her and slid his hand between her thighs, cupping her warmly. "None of the others had blond hair."

"Hawk." She spoke his name in an indrawn breath, which was the best she could do while his thumb was insolently moving across her mound. She struggled to keep her eyes open, to speak. "You called me Miranda."

His hand fell still. "What?"

"When you, uh . . . you called me Miranda." He withdrew his hand and eased away from her. His face was closed, as though a curtain had been dropped over it. "Hawk?"

"Come on, it's time to go back." He stood up and offered her his hand. She accepted it, surreptitiously grabbing her panties. She stepped into them, but Hawk didn't seem to notice her awkwardness. He was pulling on his own clothes with rapid, disjointed motions. Randy was loath to put the wet shirt back on, but she did so. When they were dressed, he took her hand again and led her back through the rock. They picked their way down the hill to his truck.

When they reached it, Randy pulled him around. "Why did you call me Miranda?"

"I didn't realize I had. Don't make a big deal of it."

"I wouldn't. But you are. It bothers you that you did. Why?"

For a moment he looked anywhere but at her. Finally he stared down into her face and said, "I wanted to be distinguished from the others."

"Others?"

"Your other lovers."

Little was said on the drive back to the compound. By the time he pulled to a stop in front of his cabin, Randy knew that he must regret what had happened at the pool. His face was closed, his lips thin with what she could only guess was disapproval of her wanton conduct. She hated seeing it, so she avoided looking at him.

He got out of the pickup first and came around to open the door for her. She alighted, but that was as far as she got because Hawk was blocking her path. She kept her eyes on the ground.

He tipped up her chin. "Obviously I didn't use a condom."

"Obviously I didn't even think about it."

After a ponderous pause, he said, "You've got nothing to worry about. I've never failed to use one before."

Everything inside her went very still. She could scarcely breathe. Inadvertently, he had told her that she was special, at least different. It wasn't much, but it was something. She would need all the justifications she could glean when she reviewed what had happened between them. "You've got nothing to worry about either, Hawk."

"You've taken care with your other lovers?"

She shook her head and blinked back large, salty tears. Wetting her lips, she answered huskily, "There've been no other lovers. None. Only my husband. And now you. I swear it."

His eyes had never gleamed so brightly. As though to shut in the light, he narrowed them on her suspiciously. After a few moments he stepped back and encircled her elbow with his hand. "Come on."

"Where?" He was leading her away from the cabin rather than toward it.

"I thought you wanted to kiss Scott good night."

She stumbled along beside him, keeping her eyes

on him rather than on the uneven path, trying to puzzle through this enigma of a man.

The mystery of Hawk O'Toole remained unsolved the next day.

After visiting with Scott for half an hour the night before, they had returned to Hawk's cabin alone. Selfishly, she was glad that Scott had remained with Ernie and Leta. He was happy to be there, and Randy was tingling with expectancy at being with Hawk alone all night.

But he didn't make love to her again, as she had thought—even hoped—that he would. They slept together in the bed. He had undressed her slowly and leisurely, only growing impatient when he began to take off his own clothes. He then pulled her beneath the covers with him and gazed at her hair where it lay on the pillow beside his. His hands moved over her body with a sculptor's sensitivity to form and texture. But he didn't even kiss her.

Once, during the night, she awakened to feel his arms tightening around her and his legs moving restlessly against hers. Her name was breathed against the back of her neck as his lips softly kissed it. She felt him full and hard against her derriere. He took it no further, however, than to close his hand around her breast and draw her closer to him. Eventually he fell asleep, and, after the time it took to reduce the thumping speed of her heart, so did she.

When she woke up, he had already left the cabin. She got up and dressed, stoked the fire, made the bed, brewed coffee. She berated herself for behaving in such a ridiculously domestic way, but every time she accidently caught her reflection in a shiny surface, she was amazed by the lambency in her eyes and the perpetual smile on her lips.

Too, there was a constant, delicious ache in her lower abdomen. Her breasts felt heavy and flushed. Her nipples were sensitive to every stimulus. Hawk hadn't satisfied her hunger; he had created it.

At the sound of the door opening, she whirled around, breathless. Hawk paused on the threshold. Their gazes held for a noticeable length of time before he came through the door. The other chiefs filed in behind him. They seemed not to notice the charged atmosphere. None but Ernie, who eyed Hawk and her shrewdly.

"Get everyone coffee," Hawk ordered harshly. Randy's spine stiffened. "Please," he added in an undertone.

She complied, not necessarily because the command had been politely amended, but because they had brought with them a newspaper. She was curious to know what the governor's reaction to receiving her bloody shirt and the accompanying letter had been.

"At least we've got his attention," Hawk reported, when he had finished reading the newspaper account of this latest development in the case. "He promises to check into the closing of the mine. He's also sidestepping Price and conferring personally with the FBI. He wants to be acquainted with every aspect of Randy and Scott's kidnapping. On the other hand, he warns that if Randy has been physically assaulted in any way, he'll exercise his authority to see that we're punished to the full extent of the law."

He glanced up at Randy. Feeling color mount in her cheeks, she lowered her eyes. She wondered if he realized that he had referred to her by her first name.

"What do we do now?" asked one member of the council.

Hawk sipped from the mug of coffee Randy had handed him. "I'm not sure. Let me think about it. We'll have another meeting this evening just before dinner and discuss our plans then. In the meantime, continue to enjoy the time off." His gaze traveled around the circle of faces. "Hopefully, we'll all be going back to work soon."

After the men left, Leta came in with Donny and Scott. The boys wrestled on the floor while Hawk and Ernie discussed their options. Randy was curious to know what they were saying, but they kept their voices low. It seemed that Hawk was pitching an idea to Ernie, but Ernie kept rejecting it. Apparently she wasn't to be consulted, so she helped Leta cook breakfast. They ate together, sitting around the table in Hawk's cabin.

The conversation flowed easily. Looking in, one would never guess that Scott and she were hostages, Randy thought. Scott asked for Hawk's help in repairing a slingshot. Along with the repair, he received a lecture on its safe usage.

"We don't have to go home yet, do we, Mommy?" Scott's question came as a total surprise. She didn't have an immediate answer.

"I . . . I don't know. Why?"

"I hope we can stay a long time. I like it here."

That said, he dashed out the door behind Donny. The adults were left to cope with an awkward silence. Leta was the one to break it. She braced her hand on Ernie's shoulder and unsteadily rose to her feet. "I don't feel well." Ernie moved faster than Randy had ever seen him. He hustled her out.

"What the hell was that all about?" Hawk demanded, as soon as Randy closed the door behind them.

"Leta's pregnant."

Hawk stared at her for a moment, then at the door, as though he could see Ernie and his young wife through the wood. Muttering a foul curse, he plowed all ten fingers through his thick, straight hair and held it away from his face. He propped his elbows on the table and rested his head in his hands.

Quietly, Randy approached him. "Aren't you happy for them?"

"Very."

"You don't seem to be."

His head came up quickly. "If Ernie is convicted of this crime, he'll go to prison."

She dropped into a chair across the table from him. "Well, welcome to the world of the clear thinking, Mr. O'Toole. That's what I've been telling you for days. You'll all go to prison."

He was shaking his head no. "I made the deal with Price. I told the others that if it didn't go as we had planned, I would take full responsibility. I made them take a blood oath that if I was arrested, they would scatter and go underground."

Randy thought that he was being generous to a fault, but she couldn't help but admire his self-sacrifice. "Your gesture is noble, still, the best they could hope for is lives as fugitives."

"That's better than prison."

"That's arguable. What about Ernie? Didn't he take the oath?"

"Yes, but he's already told me that if I go to prison, he'll surrender himself."

"I take it that Leta doesn't know that."

"I doubt she does."

He stood up and began pacing the width of the cabin. Randy cleared the breakfast dishes off the table and washed them in a basin with water from the pump that she had heated on the stove. She was so absorbed with Hawk's dilemma, she barely noticed the lack of amenities.

When she was finished, she turned to find Hawk unlocking a small metal strongbox with a tiny gold key. "What's that?"

"The Lone Puma's files. I brought them with us."

She stared at the unorganized heap of papers he dumped on the table. "That scrap pile is your filing system?"

"I'm an engineer. I know where the silver is and how to bring it out safely and economically. I also do . . . did the marketing. I'm not a bookkeeper."

"You could have hired one."

"I never got around to it." He lowered himself into a chair. "I thought there might be something here that I've overlooked, something I might use as leverage."

Again Randy sat down across the table from him. As he scanned and discarded the papers one by one, she drew them toward her and read them herself. She began to separate them into stacks, segregating tax records from payroll records, from bills of sale, from plats.

Swearing colorfully, Hawk tossed aside a copy of the contract that had transferred ownership of the Lone Puma Mine to the investors. Randy read it. It was standard as far as she could tell at first glance. The amount of money the Indians had received on the sale seemed impressive until one considered the length of time for the payout versus the potential of the mine that was being wasted.

Then, going over it more carefully, her mind snagged on one particular clause. Her heart lurched with excitement, but she carefully reread what she had just gone over to make certain she wasn't optimistically jumping to conclusions.

"Hawk, what is this?" she asked him, holding up one of the surveys of the property.

"It's a plat. Surveyors make them to determine—"

"I *know* that," she said with irritation. "I work in a surveyor's office."

That information took him completely by surprise. "You do? You work?"

"Of course I work. How do you think I support Scott and myself?"

"I figured that Price—"

"No," she said, giving her head an adamant shake, "I didn't ask for any money from him. Not even child support. I didn't want to be even that obligated. Anyway," she said, spreading the plat out on the table between them, "what is this? This area of land right here." She traced around the dotted lines on the plat that marked the area she was referring to.

Hawk's mouth curled bitterly. "It used to be open ground, pastureland where our cattle grazed."

"Cattle?"

"The tribe owned several hundred head. We raised it for beef."

"No longer?"

"No pastureland, no cattle. We lost it with the sale of the mine."

To his surprise, Randy smiled. "You mean that the new owners seized control of that land in addition to the mine?"

"There's a barbed wire fence around it now. No-trespassing signs are posted every few yards. I take that to mean they've seized control of it."

"Then they did it illegally."

His brows drew together. "What do you mean?"

"Look, that pastureland . . . several square miles, right?" She got an affirmative nod. "That land is designated on the plat, but it's not even referred to in the deed."

"Are you sure?" He couldn't contain the excitement in his voice.

"Hawk, I study plats like this all day long, checking out every detail before property changes hands. I know what I'm talking about. Those investors weren't only swindlers, they were stupid swindlers. They bought in a hurry, obviously to acquire a tax shelter at the end of the year."

She reached for his hand and pressed it. "The tribe still owns that pastureland, Hawk. And if you presented this material to the governor, I'm sure he would authorize a full investigation of the sale. Morton would be superfluous as a go-between. This," she said, slapping the contract and plat spread out in front of her, "would do you much more good than his intercession could do in a million years."

He was staring at the legal documents. "I never went over that contract with a fine-tooth comb. Damn! I was too angry. Every time I thought about it, it made me sick to my stomach. I couldn't bring myself to even look at it."

"Don't blame yourself for past negligence. Just act on the information now. Hindsight is better than no sight at all." Randy watched him gather up all the papers and stuff them back into the strongbox, undoing all the careful categorizing Randy had done. "Your filing system still leaves a lot to be desired."

He merely gave her a lopsided grin. Relocking the strongbox and tucking it beneath his arm, he came around the table. As he drew up beside Randy, he gripped a handful of her hair and pulled her head up and back. "Tell me about the lovers."

Her gaze didn't waver. "I told you last night. There were none. They didn't exist."

"Why didn't you deny the nasty allegations?"

"Why should I? They were untrue. I refused to

honor them with denials. Morton had the lovers. He was unfaithful to me almost from the beginning of our marriage. After he won his congressional seat, he seemed to think that extra women were his due, a bonus he was entitled to take. He flaunted his affairs in my face, knowing that I wanted to keep the family intact for Scott's sake. When I finally had my fill of it and couldn't tolerate his infidelity another day, I demanded a divorce. He threatened to file for sole custody of Scott if I divorced him on the grounds of adultery. That wouldn't have been good for his image."

"He would never have gotten custody of the boy."

"Probably not. But I didn't want to put Scott through a well-publicized, messy trial like that, and Morton knew it. Besides, I wasn't absolutely confident that I would win. He had enough friends in high places lined up to testify under oath that I'd slept with them, seduced them."

"What friends?"

"Men who owed Morton political favors."

"When I accused you of being a faithless wife, why didn't you deny it? Why did you let me torment you?"

"When Morton began leaking gossip about my many affairs, my own mother only said tsk-tsk and reprimanded me for not being more discreet. I didn't deny it to her either. If she was willing to believe that kind of lie about me, I was willing to let her. Since she obviously had very little faith in me, I ceased to care what she thought about me."

"Then why did you tell *me*?"

The unspoken answer vibrated between them. Hawk's opinion of her mattered a great deal.

His fingers had maintained a tight grip on her hair. Her arching neck should have felt the strain, but it didn't. She felt only the heat of Hawk's eyes pouring over her face. He applied a slight, unintentional pressure to the back of her head, drawing her face closer to his lap. Instinctively, Randy raised her hand and laid it high on his thigh. He released an involuntary groan.

Between choppy breaths he said, "If you keep looking at me like that, you'll have to—"

The knock on the door broke them apart. Randy quickly withdrew her hand. Hawk released his grip on her hair and stepped back. "Come in."

His voice was as dark as his unwavering eyes, which held her stare. Ernie stepped through the door and assessed the situation at one glance. The air crackled with electric sexuality. "I can come back later," he said, retracing his steps through the open doorway.

"No," Hawk said. "I was coming to look for you. We've got a lot to talk about."

He didn't even lock the cabin door behind him when he left.

Eleven

The mood around the bonfire that night was almost festive. The tribal council had a plan that would restore the mine to them. The people didn't know exactly what the plan was, nor did they care. They merely trusted the council to come through for them. All the chiefs, but especially Hawk, were treated with more respect and deference than usual.

Johnny approached Hawk's blanket while he and Randy were eating. Since the day of her aborted escape attempt, every time she'd seen the young man, he'd been diligently at work, as though trying to redeem himself for his previous negligence. Now, he held out his hands parallel to the ground. They were no longer shaking. "I've been sober for three days," he said.

Hawk didn't crack a smile, but the young man wouldn't have expected him to. "You've done a fine job on the trucks and restored my confidence in you. When we return to the mine, the specialized equipment will need to be overhauled. I'll appoint you permanent overseer of the garage if you'll agree to attend a mechanics school in the city. The tribe would pay for your tuition. Are you interested?"

"Yes."

Hawk gave him an appraising stare. "I'll check into it as soon as possible." Johnny's dark eyes glowed, but he said no more before leaving them. He didn't wander off by himself as before, but mingled with the others. Randy saw him approach one of the young women and hesitantly strike up a conversation with her.

"I think his broken heart and wounded ego are on the mend."

Hawk absently agreed, but his attention had already been diverted to the couple approaching them, walking hand in hand. The handsome young man was standing proud and tall, but the woman was demurely keeping her eyes on the ground in front of her.

"Welcome back, Aaron," Hawk said to the man.

"I'm only here for two days. I've registered, but I don't actually start classes until Monday."

"You had enough money to pay for everything?"

The young man nodded. He glanced down at the girl and for the first time began to show signs of nervousness. He wet his lips before speaking to Hawk again. "I'd like your permission to marry Dawn January."

Hawk's eyes moved to Dawn. She looked at him briefly, then cast her gaze downward again. "What about school?"

"I graduate in May," Aaron reminded him. "We'd like to marry next June. Next fall, we'd like for Dawn to enroll in college and get her degree also."

"This is something you need to bring before the council."

"I wanted to this afternoon, but didn't because I

knew the other matters under discussion were so pressing." He glanced at Randy. "I've privately consulted with all the other chiefs on the council. They've granted their permission."

"Is Dawn's family agreeable?"

"Yes."

"And she?"

The young man pulled her forward slightly. She spoke in a soft bride's voice. "I want to marry Aaron Turnbow."

"Then you have my permission," Hawk said. "But not until you graduate, Aaron," he qualified hastily.

They thanked him with proper deference, then turned and rushed off. Before the darkness swallowed them up, Randy and Hawk saw Dawn cross her arms behind her fiance's neck and plaster her body against his.

"I doubt they'll wait until June to consummate it."

"I doubt they'll wait until morning. Not if Dawn has anything to say about it," Randy remarked snidely.

Hawk's head came around quickly. His stern face tried to hold back a smile at her catty comment. "I just hope he doesn't get her pregnant and force me to move the wedding date up by several months. We've invested heavily in Aaron's college education. So far he's lived up to our expectations. I was afraid he would meet an anglo girl at college and—"

"What?" Randy asked, when he came to an abrupt and incomplete end to his sentence.

"Nothing."

"And what?" she persisted.

"And want to marry her."

"Would that have been so terrible?" Her heart was hurting. She didn't want to hear his answer, but knew that she must.

"We need strong, intelligent young men like Aaron. If he had married a white woman, in all probability he would have left the tribe."

"And never been welcomed back," she said quietly, adding what he had deliberately omitted.

"He could have lived on the reservation, but he couldn't have held a position on the council. It's very difficult, if not impossible, to straddle two cultures. Once you choose, it's a lifetime choice."

He turned his head away. Randy studied his profile, which was cast in relief against the mellow glow of the fire. He was a tough, but fair, leader. She admired his sense of justice. His chastisements were subtle, but effective. Because his praise was rare, it was valued greatly. He took to heart the problems of each member of his tribe. She was glad she had met this one man, in her entire lifetime, who wasn't always looking out for number one. Until she knew Hawk O'Toole, she hadn't thought that one existed.

But as she continued to watch him, something occurred to her. Hawk was alone. Even though he sat amidst people who obviously revered him, he was removed from them. There was a separateness about him that caused her heartache. Sadness lurked in the depths of his blue eyes. He kept it carefully screened, but in unguarded moments it became apparent to anyone looking for it. For his unhappy childhood and the guilt he bore, he suffered in silence and he suffered alone.

Before she could closely examine the emotions churning inside her, Scott appeared and sat down on the blanket beside her.

"Hi, Mommy." Uncharacteristically glum, he snuggled close and laid his head on her chest.

"Hello, darling. Where have you been? I haven't seen you for a while. What have you been up to?"

"Nothing."

She looked at Hawk inquiringly, but he shrugged, indicating that he didn't know what had brought on Scott's melancholia. "Is something wrong?"

"No," Scott grumbled.

"Are you sure?"

"Yeah, only . . ."

"Only?"

He sat up. "Only Donny's getting a new baby."

"I know. I think that's wonderful news. Don't you?"

"I guess, but he's telling everybody." He made a broad sweeping gesture with his hands, as though encompassing the world. "He said I wasn't getting one. Can we get one too, Mommy? Please?"

For a moment the request rendered her speechless, then she laughed softly and gave him the universal parental put-off. "We'll see."

"That's what you said about the bunny rabbit, and I never got to get a bunny rabbit. I promise I'll help you take care of the baby. Please."

"Scott."

The boy's earnest pleadings ceased abruptly when Hawk spoke his name. "Sir?"

"Where's your knife?" Scott pulled it from his belt. Hawk took it, studying it as it lay in his palm. "You haven't lost it again?" Obviously when he had returned the knife to Scott, he hadn't told him that his mother had taken it from him while they were hugging.

"No, sir."

"Hmm. I think you deserve a reward for taking such good care of this knife. A scabbard."

"It's already got a scabbard, Hawk."

"But not like this one." From his shirt pocket, Hawk removed a tooled leather scabbard. He slid the knife into it and handed both back to Scott, who accepted them with a reverence reserved for holy relics.

"Gee, Hawk. It's neat. Where'd you get it?"

"From my grandfather. He made it for me when I was about your age. I want you to keep it."

To remember me by. He didn't say that, but Randy heard the words in her head, spoken in Hawk's voice. The gift seemed like a going-away present. The thought caused her heart to flutter in panic, which made no sense at all. Hadn't she tried to get away only a few days ago? Now the thought of leaving and never seeing Hawk O'Toole again was a dismal one. What had brought on this reversal?

Before she had time to muddle through it, Leta and Ernie approached with Donny, who was so impressed with the scabbard, he stopped bragging about his awaited sibling.

"Do you want Scott to stay in our cabin again tonight?" Ernie asked, looking from Hawk to Randy and back again.

"You've got more room in your cabin than I do in mine," Hawk observed. "It would make better sense for that reason."

"He and his mother could stay in the cabin they occupied when they got here."

Ernie's alternative didn't meet with Hawk's approval. "The stove hasn't been lit in days. It will be too cold."

"Scott is no trouble at all," Leta said, unaware of the underlying tension. She shepherded the boys away. Ernie, looking like he had more to say but thinking better of it, followed his family.

"I don't think Ernie likes me," Randy said, after they were out of earshot.

In one smooth motion and without using his hands, Hawk came to his feet and helped Randy to stand. Together they started walking through the compound toward his cabin. "Ernie doesn't like anglo women in general."

"I gathered that."

"He thinks they're aggressive and too smart for their own good."

"We're not submissive enough."

"That sort of sums it up."

"What do you think?"

"I think Ernie is a lost cause as far as the feminist movement goes."

"I mean, what do you think about anglo women?"

"Any one in particular?" By now they had reached the cabin. He firmly shut the door just as he asked the question.

Randy turned to face him. "What do you think about me?"

He advanced into the room until only inches were separating them. "I haven't finished forming my opinion of you yet."

"First impression?" she asked coquettishly.

"I wanted you in bed."

She sucked in her breath. "Oh."

The only light in the room was coming from the fire burning in the stove. Graceful shadows danced across the rough log walls, across the floor, across the two people staring into each other's eyes.

For a long while, that's all they did. Then, moving with painstaking slowness, Hawk put his hands in her hair and combed his fingers through it. He lifted it off her neck and held it out at the sides of her head, watching the firelight filter through the blond strands. "You've got beautiful hair, especially in firelight."

Randy found it difficult to speak, but she said a gruff thank you.

Hawk cupped her face between his hands and ran his thumbs along her lower eyelashes. "You've got eyes the color of the first leaves of spring."

He slid his hands down to her neck and momentarily closed his fingers around it before letting them move down to her chest. She had been given a fresh shirt that morning. It was no more attractive than its predecessors. Hawk didn't seem to notice. He seemed more interested in the way she gave shape to the front of it. The manner in which he looked at her made her feel more beautiful than she had ever felt.

His hands glided over the soft mounds of her breasts. "Take it off," he said, lowering his hands to his sides.

She ducked her head only once and that was to locate the top button. After that, holding his gaze, she undid the buttons and peeled off the shirt. She dropped it to the floor. She saw Hawk swallow, saw his hand reaching for her, but her eyes had already closed by the time he touched her.

"Beautiful breasts." He cupped her gingerly. "Beautiful, sensitive nipples." He let out a long, raspy breath when her nipples hardened against his caressing fingertips. Lowering his head, he stroked one of them with the tip of his tongue. Randy's stomach quivered and she moaned softly. He continued the love play, encircling the rigid crests with his nimble tongue until they were distended so far they almost touched him.

Which was obviously what he wanted. He rapidly unbuttoned his shirt and shrugged it off, unable to get rid of it fast enough. Placing his strong, dark hands in the center of her back, he drew her against him. Her breasts left damp impressions on his chest. Groaning his pleasure at the sight, he lowered his head and kissed her. It wasn't a hard, demanding kiss, but deep and questing, as though he wanted to touch her soul with his searching tongue.

They continued to nuzzle each other, rubbing noses and cheeks and chins and lips together. Randy soon realized why he wasn't embracing her. He was unbuttoning his jeans. When they were undone, he took a step away from her.

Their breathing was unsteady and swift as they looked at each other. Finally Randy's eyes lowered to his chest. It was incredibly smooth and sleek, marvelously formed of muscle and bone and skin. Her fingertip traced the line that squared off his pectoral muscle. When she reached the sternum, she followed the shallow indentation down, over his ridged stomach, beyond his narrow waist, to the ribbon of dark, glossy hair. She traced it into the dimple of his navel. There she dallied, wondering what was expected of her.

She didn't have to wait long to find out. Hawk took her hand and moved it into the open wedge of his jeans. But he left the decision up to her by removing his hand and leaving hers, open, against him.

Randy closed her eyes and inclined forward. She turned her head to one side and laid her cheek against his chest. Only then did she slide her hand into the dense thatch of hair. When she touched him, he shuddered. When she cupped him and lifted him up and out, he cried, "Miranda," and wrapped his arms around her.

She tilted her head back to receive his tempestuous kiss. He reached beneath her skirt and rid her of underpants. He then gathered the fabric of her skirt in his hands and tilted her hips toward his.

They touched; the contact was more than they could stand.

Hawk moved to the bed. He sat, half reclining, against the wall behind it and pulled her over his lap. With his hands supporting her hips, he drew her body toward his mouth and kissed her through her skirt. Lifting it, he kissed her belly, her smooth thighs, the patch of tawny hair between them. He sank lower, continually kissing, separating and investigating the silky furrows of her femininity with his tongue.

Almost instantly Randy reached a shuddering, heart-stopping climax. Before she had fully recovered, he lowered her hips and impaled her upon his rigid heat. Their lips met in a fierce and hungry kiss. His hands, applying subtle pressure to her hips, guided her motions.

Desperately wanting to please him, she shed any and all inhibitions and gave more than he asked for. Their bodies were shiny with perspiration and hot with fever when they surrendered to the passion that threatened to consume them.

Replete, barely having the energy to move, they separated long enough to remove the rest of their clothing. Hawk then drew her naked form against his and pulled a blanket over them.

"Ernie wouldn't approve," she whispered against his neck.

"The hell with Ernie." His chuckle vibrated in her ear.

Her smile of satiation faded upon reflection of what had just transpired. "Hawk, I don't want you to compromise your position in the tribe because of me."

He tipped her head up. "Nothing that has happened tonight will make a difference."

"You're sure?"

"Positive."

"But I thought that if—"

"Shh." He lightly ran his thumb over her lower lip. "Your mouth is bruised."

"From kissing you so hard."

"I'm sorry I hurt you."

"I'm not." She inched up and pressed her lips over his. They shared a long, sweet, melding kiss while his roving hands cherished her.

Randy remembered little else after that. Sprawled across his chest, with her hair covering his copper skin and his heart beating out a cadence in her ear, she slipped into sleep.

She was awakened by the absence of his body heat. Before opening her eyes, she tried to snuggle closer. Her hands reached for him, but came up empty. She opened her eyes and discovered herself alone in the bed. Startled, she swung her head around. She lay back down, relieved to have spotted him standing at the window. His shoulder was propped against the sill. He was staring through the window pane, unmoving.

He was still naked, seemingly impervious to the chill in the room. Drawing the covers up over her shoulders, Randy took advantage of his lack of awareness to watch him. His shoulders were broad, his torso long and beautifully proportioned. His buttocks were taut and narrow, gracefully swelling out from the small of his back. He had long thighs and sinewy calves. Arms, hands, feet—she couldn't find a single flaw.

She admired his body as one of God's finest creations. As a woman, she desired it. It was capable of giving her incredible pleasure, of coaxing feelings and sensations from her that she hadn't known were there. He had brought to life erogenous parts of her body that had lain dormant since she was born. He exercised a powerful and wonderful magic over her body.

Brimming with emotion, Randy eased back the covers and padded over to him. She moved up behind him and pressed the front of her body against his back, then slipped her hands beneath his arms and crossed them over his chest.

"Good morning," she said, pecking a kiss on his shoulder blade.

"Good morning."

"What are you doing up so early?"

"Couldn't sleep."

"Why didn't you wake me?"

"There was no need to."

Maybe she should have left him to his private thoughts. He wasn't in a talkative, receptive mood. But she didn't want to return to the bed that seemed so empty without him. "What are you looking at?"

"The sky."

"What are you thinking about?"

His chest rose and fell with a deep sigh, though he didn't make a sound. "My life, my mother, father, the brother who was stillborn. My grandfather. The Irishman who took an Indian girl for his wife and left me with anglo eyes."

She wanted to tell him what stunning eyes they were, but she was certain he already knew. She was also certain how he felt about their distinctiveness. "You resent your eyes because they're not Indian, don't you?"

He shrugged indifferently, but she strongly sensed that her guess was right. She kissed his spine and splayed her hands on his stomach. Slowly she let them coast down. They skimmed his lean hipbones, sifted through his body hair, glanced his sex, before moving to the tops of his thighs. She felt his body tense, but he didn't overtly respond.

"You're beautiful, Hawk O'Toole. All of you is beautiful."

Her hands began moving back up, only this time her touch was less analytical and more sexual. Suddenly, he caught her hands and held them still. "Go back to bed," he said in a harsh, curt voice. "It's cold."

Randy uttered a small cry of dismay and quickly withdrew her hands. Feeling brutally rejected, she spun away. Before she had taken two steps, however, his hand closed around her wrist and drew her up.

"You think I don't want you." It was a statement rather than a question. "I don't," he growled.

Randy had no time to react before he lifted her against his lap, braced her against the wall, and thrust himself into her. Palm to palm, their hands were flattened against the wall on either side of her head. Burying his face in her hair, he ground his hips against hers.

He moaned. "Oh, dear Lord. I don't want to want you, but I do. I don't want you because you make me weak."

At first overwhelmed, Randy encircled his waist with her legs and drew him closer. Reflexively, her hips began to move.

"No, don't move," he said raggedly. "Don't . . . don't do anything but hold me tight inside you. Make it last. Glove me. Just let me feel you surrounding me. Let me stay . . . Oh, no, no . . ." The staggering words gave way to the warm jetting tide.

His groan of release was low and long and tinged with desperation.

Some minutes later, he set her on her feet. Randy searched his averted face for an explanation. She wasn't offended. She was perplexed. Her bewilderment was tinged with fear, but of what she couldn't say. Before she could press Hawk for meanings behind his behavior, she heard noises that were out of keeping with the breaking dawn.

Going to the window, she looked out. The rising sun was just spreading its glow over the mountainside. The figures alighting from the convoy of cars below looked like black insects as they scurried about over the rocky ground.

"Hawk!" she cried out in alarm. "It's the police. How'd they get here? How'd they find us?"

"I sent for them."

Twelve

"You sent for them! *Why*?"

He reached for his jeans and pulled them on. "To turn myself in." He broke the news to her without any expression of emotion either in his face or his voice. "You'd better get dressed. They'll expect you down there soon."

"Hawk!" she cried, grabbing his arm and forcing him to look at her. "What is going on? Why are you doing this? I thought you were going to send the deed to the governor."

He shook off her hand and began tossing her clothing at her piece by piece. "A copy was delivered to his office yesterday. After giving him a few hours to read over it, I called him."

"You talked to him directly?"

"It took some doing, but after I made a few veiled threats regarding your life, he agreed to speak to me."

"Well, what did he say?" she asked impatiently, when he turned his back to her and started pulling on the rest of his clothing.

"He said he would give the matter his full consideration, *if* I surrendered myself to the authorities and released you and Scott. I agreed, but only if he would guarantee that I would be the only one held accountable for your kidnapping. He gave me that guarantee."

"Hawk," she said miserably, clutching her clothes to her chest. "That's not fair."

"Not much in life is. Now, get dressed."

"But—"

"Put your clothes on, unless you want me to drag you naked down to the gate. I don't think your ex-husband would appreciate that." He hadn't behaved in this hard and uncompromising way since that first night at the temporary camp just after the actual kidnapping. His jaw was rigid with resolve, his eyes glittering with hatred.

"What role does Morton play in your surrender?"

"I don't know, but he's sure to be waiting there with open arms to welcome Scott and you back."

"You want me . . . *us* . . . to go back to him?"

His eyes were cold and unfeeling as he said, "I couldn't care less. You were a pleasant diversion while you were here. Nice to look at. Nice to feel. Nice to . . ." He hitched his chin in the direction of the rumpled bed. "If it's true that you never had lovers before or since your divorce, your talents were being wasted."

Randy's chest heaved with the need to cry out in emotional agony, but she contained it. Giving him her back, she clamped her teeth over her lower lip. Her coordination was so bad she could barely pull on her clothes. When she was finally dressed, she turned to him. He was holding the door open, his face stony.

At the end of the path leading to the cabin, Ernie

was waiting with Scott. The little boy's eyes were still puffy with sleepiness. They were also troubled. As she and Hawk approached, he ran to her.

"Mommy, Ernie says I gotta go home now. I don't, do I? Can't I stay longer?"

She took his hand and gave him a watery smile. "I'm afraid you can't, Scott. It's past time for us to leave."

"But I don't want to go home yet. I want to stay and play with Donny. I want to see his baby brother when he gets borned."

"Scott."

The single word from Hawk stopped his flow of whining protests. "But, Hawk, I—"

One look into Hawk's unblinking eyes silenced him. Dejected, Scott lowered his head and stood subdued at Randy's side. Ernie stepped directly in Hawk's path.

"Let me go with you," he said.

"We've been over this a hundred times. Don't be foolish. You'll be needed here to take care of your sons. See that they grow up smart and strong. Make them men of conviction and purpose."

Ernie's lined face seemed to stretch longer. Sadly, he laid his hand on Hawk's shoulder. They shared a long, telling stare. At last Ernie dropped his arm and stepped aside.

With Randy and Scott leading the way, the procession started down the central street of the compound toward the gate. Randy was aware of eyes, solemn and bleak, watching them from behind window panes. Beyond the gate, officially marked cars from the capitol city formed an intimidating semicircle. She recognized the man standing in its center as the governor of the state. And next to him, Morton. At the sight of him, she wanted to retch.

"That's Daddy," Scott remarked on a low, disinterested voice.

"Yes."

"How come he's here?"

"I guess he missed you and wanted to see you."

Scott said nothing. Nor did he increase his pace in anticipation of seeing his father. If anything, his footsteps became more laggardly.

"Mommy, what are all these policemen doing here? I'm scared."

"There's nothing for you to be afraid of, Scott. They want to give you a police escort home, that's all."

"What's that?"

"It's something they only do for very important people, like the president."

"Oh." The idea of a police escort didn't seem to excite him either.

Before they reached the gate, Hawk halted. Randy turned and looked at him, her eyes bleak and questioning.

"They're expecting you to come ahead of me. I asked them to take you and Scott away before I'm arrested. For the boy's sake."

Hawk in handcuffs, being stuffed into the backseat of a police car. Inwardly, she shuddered to think of Scott witnessing that. "I'm glad you thought of it. That's best, of course."

Despite the harsh words he had said to her earlier, Randy's heart was tearing in two. She wanted to memorize his face. This might be the last time she would see it set against its natural setting, against the sky, which was the very color of his eyes, against the mountainside, which was as rugged and indomitable as his profile.

His body was as tall and lean as the evergreens in

the background. The wind lifted his hair and she was reminded of the black, glossy wings of a magnificent bird of prey.

"Hawk, aren't you coming with us?" Scott asked him in a quavering voice. Even if he didn't understand the repercussions of what was happening, he sensed that something was amiss.

"No, Scott. I've got some business to do with these men, but not until after you leave."

"I'd rather just stay with you."

"You can't."

"Please," he asked, his voice cracking.

A muscle in Hawk's cheek twitched, but he maintained his proud posture. "Where are your knife and scabbard?"

Scott, his eyes shimmering with tears and his lower lip trembling, touched them where they were attached to his belt.

"Good. I'm depending on you to watch over your mother."

"I promise I will."

He clasped Scott's shoulder firmly, much as Ernie had bid him good-bye, then he withdrew his hand and stepped back quickly, as though severing an invisible cord. He gave Randy a piercing stare. "Go on. Before they become impatient."

There were a thousand things she needed and wanted to say, had she the time to say them and had Hawk wanted to hear them. Drawing from an inner resource of strength, she turned, bringing a reluctant Scott around with her.

Together they moved through the gate. Morton rushed forward and gripped her shoulders. "Randy, are you all right? Did he make good his threats and hurt you?"

"Get your hands off me," she spat.

Morton blinked at her in astonishment, but to save face with all the spectators, he complied. "Scott? Scott, are you all right, son?"

"I'm fine, Daddy. How come I have to go home now?"

"Wha—"

"Governor Adams?" Randy addressed him.

The statesman had been blessed with oratory skills and a keen political mind to make up for an unimpressive, paunchy physique and prematurely balding head. He stepped forward. "Yes, Mrs. Price? What can I do for you?" he said, taking her hand. "I realize that you've been through a terrible ordeal. Anything I can do to help you, you've only got to ask."

"Thank you. Will you please instruct those officers to put their guns away?"

Governor Adams momentarily lost his composure. He had expected a request for food, water, fresh clothing, medical attention, protection. Randy's request took him totally off guard.

"Mrs. Price, they have their weapons drawn for your protection. We couldn't rely on Mr. O'Toole's promise to deliver you unharmed."

"Why not?" she demanded. "Do we look harmed in any way?"

"Well, no, but—"

"Didn't Mr. O'Toole give you his word that he wouldn't harm us?" It was a lucky guess, and by the embarrassment on the governor's face, a correct one.

"Yes, he did."

"Then have the weapons put away or I'm not moving from this spot. The guns are frightening my son."

Morton propped his hands on his hips. "Randy, just what the hell do you think—"

"Do not address me in that condescending tone of voice, Morton."

"Yeah," Scott piped up. "Hawk'll get mad at you if you yell at Mommy."

"Now see here—"

Governor Adams held up his hand. "Please, Mr. Price. Apparently Mrs. Price has something to say."

"That's right. I do. The guns?"

Adams gave her a measuring stare. He glanced beyond her shoulder to the man standing above them on a ledge of rock outlined against the sky. With a wave of his hand, he summoned the senior FBI agent forward. They held a brief and furtive discussion. Randy had to argue her point with him just as she had done with the governor, but finally the order was given for all weapons to be put away. Only after she saw that they were did the knot of tension in her chest begin to loosen.

"Yesterday, did you receive a folder of Xeroxed material from Mr. O'Toole?"

"Indeed I did," Governor Adams replied. "Very interesting reading."

"And didn't you speak with him by telephone regarding this material and an ensuing investigation?"

"I did."

"Then there is no call for all this." She spread her hand wide to encompass the patrol cars.

"The man has agreed to surrender himself to the authorities."

"For what?"

"For what?" Morton exclaimed. "He committed a federal crime."

"He executed it. Who *planned* it?" she fired at him. Morton went whey-faced. While he was temporarily rendered dumb, Randy turned back to the governor, whose brows were drawn together in disapproval and suspicion. "Governor Adams, Morton is ultimately responsible for this entire incident. He duped Mr. O'Toole into thinking that conditions on the reservation could be improved upon and that the Lone Puma Mine would be restored to the tribe if he did Morton this little 'favor.' Needless to say, Morton had no one's interest at heart except his own. He instigated this kidnapping for the publicity it would give him before the election in November."

The governor's glower could have turned Morton to stone. It said that he would be dealt with properly later. In the meantime he wanted to proceed with matters at hand.

"The fact still remains, Mrs. Price, that Mr. O'Toole kidnapped you and your son off that train."

"If he's prosecuted, I'll swear that he didn't. I'll testify that we went with him willingly," she said staunchly.

"He stole money from one of the passengers."

"He took money that was practically pressed into his hand by a loudmouth who thought he was being cute. When witnesses are put on the stand, they'll have to testify to that. Everyone thought the 'holdup' was a hoax. No one was in any danger. Ever."

"No one but you and your son."

"Never," she said, shaking her head adamantly.

"I received a ripped shirt with your blood on it."

She held up her wounded thumb. "A kitchen accident," she lied. "The shirt didn't belong to me." That was sidestepping the truth. "Putting my blood on it and sending it to you was a desperation move on Mr. O'Toole's part to gain your attention. We were never in any real physical danger. Ask Scott."

Governor Adams looked down at Scott, who was following the conversation as well as his limited vocabulary would allow. The governor knelt down and said, "Scott, were you ever afraid of the Indians?"

He screwed up his face and thought back. "A little, when I first got on the horse with Ernie, but he kept telling he that he wouldn't let me go. Then I was kinda scared of Geronimo 'cause he kept trying to butt me with his head."

"Geronimo is a goat," Randy said for clarification.

"I still don't like him very much," Scott admitted.

"Did Mr. O'Toole ever hurt you? Or threaten to hurt you?"

Puzzled by the question, Scott shook his head. "No. Hawk's neat." He glanced over his shoulder and happily waved at the stalwart silhouette. "He's not waving back 'cause he doesn't like all those cars parked on the grass and making trails. He says that sometimes men do bad things to the land. That's why they mine the silver the way they do so it doesn't mess up anything on top of the ground."

The governor was obviously impressed by what he heard, but he asked Scott one last question. "Did Mr. O'Toole ever hurt your mother?"

Scott shaded his eyes against the sun and looked up at her. "No. But he had a knife—"

"A knife?"

"This one." Scott pulled the knife from its new scabbard. "He gave it to me and said that if he ever did hurt my mommy, I could stab him in the heart with it. He never did though, so I didn't have to stab him. I don't think I would anyway, 'cause Hawk said that knives are okay to skin animals and gut fish, but I shouldn't ever turn it on a person."

Morton rounded on Randy. "You let my kid play with knives? You want him to be as savage as your new lover?" he asked nastily, flinging his hand toward Hawk. He reached for the knife. "Give me that thing."

"*No!*" Scott screamed, and bent double to protect the knife.

Morton lunged for him and roughly grabbed his small arm.

Hawk leaped from the shelf of rock and came racing forward. Automatic weapons, which had been previously concealed, were snapped into place again and aimed at him.

"Don't fire!" Governor Adams yelled, holding up his hands.

After a tense moment, Governor Adams turned to Randy. "Mrs. Price, you've been most instrumental in clearing up this"—he paused and shot Morton a scathing look—"disgraceful misunderstanding. But I'm afraid I can't just dismiss the issue."

"Why not?"

"This episode has cost the taxpayers a tremendous amount of money."

"So will needlessly arresting Mr. O'Toole."

"The public will demand a satisfactory explanation."

"I'm certain you can rise to the occasion, Governor Adams. Think what an opportunity it will be for you to rally support for the Indians' cause, which I'm certain you feel strongly about."

He assessed her shrewdly. "Very well, I give you my word that I'll look into the Puma Mine swindle immediately. Now, may I offer you and your son a ride back to the capitol in my limousine?"

"Thank you, Governor, but we're not going back."

"You mean we can stay?" Scott cried. "Oh, boy, can I go tell Donny?" Without waiting for permission, he brushed past his father and charged through the gate.

Morton sputtered, but Adams silenced him with a brusque wave of his hand and turned his attention back to Randy. "In that case, will you deliver a message to Mr. O'Toole?"

"Gladly."

"Tell him that I'll arrange a meeting with repre
sentatives from the Inter-Tribal Council, the BIA
lawyers from my office, and the current owners o
the mine. I'm sure an IRS agent would like to be in
on that meeting too. As soon as we designate a time
and place, I'll be in touch with him. In the mean
time I suggest that he return to the village near the
Lone Puma."

She gripped his hand. "Thank you very much
Governor Adams. Thank you."

She didn't even give Morton a backward glance
though he called her a dirty name as she went pas
him. The epithet, his disdain, didn't matter to he
in the least. She kept her eyes trained on the man
standing just inside the gate. Her heart was beating
wildly, but her footsteps were sure and unfaltering
as she moved toward him.

When only inches separated them, she looked into
his stern face and said, "You took me off that train
by force, so you're stuck with me. I know you desire
me. I suspect you even love me, though you don'
want to admit it. More than anything, you *need* me
Hawk O'Toole. You need me to hold you in the night
when you're alone. You need my reinforcement when
you're in doubt. You need my love. And I need yours."

His face remained impassive. She wet her lips
nervously. "Besides that, you're going to make me
look like a damn fool if you send me back now."

She saw a flicker of amusement in his eyes. He
moved, reaching out and gathering a handful of her
hair in his fist. He wound it around until he con
trolled the movement of her head. Then he drew her
mouth up to his for a scorching kiss.

EPILOGUE

"Isn't he beautiful?"

Randy smoothed the crown of her newborn son's head. It was covered with straight, dark hair.

"For a half-breed, he's okay."

She swatted Hawk's caressing finger away from the baby's cheek. "Don't you dare say that about my son."

"*Our* son," her husband corrected with an affectionate smile. He replaced his finger against the baby's cheek. It puffed in and out as he vigorously suckled his mother's breast. "He is beautiful, isn't he?"

Hawk's face was filled with wonder and awe. His visage was normally stern. That hadn't changed. But contrary to a year ago, his features softened more frequently now—when he laughed at Scott's antics, when he made love to Randy, when their eyes met in a public place and they could only communicate their love silently.

"He certainly is, but I already see strains of your temperament in him." She pulled the infant away

from her breast. His balled fist boxed the air and h
newborn features contorted with fierce displeasur
"Relax, you're only done on that side," Randy scolde
gently, as she transferred him to her other breas
He latched onto the nipple and started suckin
noisily.

Hawk smiled at the gusto his son demonstrated
"If he keeps eating like that, he's going to grow up
be a halfback."

"I thought Scott was going to be a halfback."

"There are two on every offensive team. We coul
have two more sons and round out the whole back
field. We'll sell them to the highest-bidding NFL team

"Do I have anything to say about this?"

"You could say no every night when I reach fo
you." He leaned down and brushed a kiss across he
lips. "But you never do."

She lowered her lashes. "How indelicate of you t
point that out, Mr. O'Toole."

Just then a hospital nurse came in carrying
vase of roses. "More flowers," she said to Randy
setting them on the nightstand. "How are we doin
here?" She peered over Hawk's shoulder.

"I believe he's finally full." Randy gazed down a
her son lovingly. He had stopped sucking and wa
sleeping contentedly.

"I'll take him back to the nursery."

"Just a minute." Hawk slipped his hands under
neath his son and lifted him up. He pressed a so
kiss on the baby's forehead, nuzzled his cheek, an
admired the sleeping face and strong limbs befor
passing the child to the nurse.

He escorted them to the door as though seein
them safely on their way back to the nursery. Whe
he turned toward the bed, he was alarmed to fin
Randy's eyes cloudy with tears. "What's the matter?

She sniffed. "Nothing. I was just thinking how much I love you." He sat down and kissed her softly. "That kiss is from Scott, who wants to know when you're bringing his baby brother home."

"Tell him only two more days. How is he?"

"Busy working on a drawing for you, which he promised should be finished by tomorrow."

She smiled. "I'll look forward to that. Who are the flowers from?"

He read the attached card. "Ernie and Leta. I'm sure they were Leta's idea. Ernie's chapped because my son weighed more at birth than his."

"How well I know." Wincing, she laid a hand on her unfamiliarly flat tummy.

"Are you in pain?" Hawk asked, his mouth tensing. Because his mother had died as a result of childbirth, he'd been anxious over Randy's health all through her pregnancy. The day he drove her into the city to the hospital, he'd been far more concerned about the delivery than Randy herself had been.

"No, I'm not in pain," she assured him. "I was only teasing."

She brushed a strand of hair off his forehead. For a while after they were married, she had been hesitant to openly express her affection for him except when they were in bed. Soon, however, she had discovered that Hawk enjoyed her spontaneous caresses, probably because he'd experienced so little affection in his lifetime.

"Ernie still doesn't like me," she said, glancing at the roses.

"You're my wife."

"Meaning?"

"If a woman doesn't reside in his kitchen and his bed, he's indifferent to her. You mistake his indifference for dislike. I know that he respects you in spite of himself."

"His attitude toward me improved—marginally—when he became convinced that I wasn't going to lure you away from the reservation."

He stroked her neck with the backs of his fingers. "He could see that first night I climbed into the pickup with you and held a knife at your throat just how powerful a lure you could have been."

Giving birth had left her emotionally tremulous. On the brink of tears again, she steered the conversation away from their personal life. "I'm proud of their new house for Leta. They needed the additional space for their growing family."

"They've prospered this year. We all have. Thanks to you for restoring the mine to us," he added quietly.

"I only set things in motion. It was your power of persuasion that made them happen."

He braced his arm on the pillow behind her head and leaned over her. "Have I thanked you?"

"At least a million times."

"Thanks, one more time." He kissed her sweetly, chastely. "That kiss is from me."

"I thought I felt your special touch behind it."

"Have I mentioned how much I miss you, how empty my bed is without you, how much I love you?"

"Not today."

He kissed her again, keeping it innocent, until her tongue came in search of his. With a moan of longing, his mouth sank down upon hers. His hand moved to her gown and opened it. He covered her breast fondly and possessively. When he felt the sticky moisture, he raised his head and gazed down at her. "I love to watch my son nurse."

"I know. I love watching you watch him."

Hawk lightly stroked her dusky nipple and a bead of milk formed on the pad of his thumb. "He didn't drink it all. You've still got milk."

"Plenty," she replied huskily.

His inquiring eyes flew up to hers. They held for several misty seconds. Then Randy lovingly curved her hand around the back of his head and drew it down.

THE EDITOR'S CORNER

We sail into our LOVESWEPT summer with six couples who, at first glance, seem to be unlikely matches. What they all have in common, and the reason that everything works out in the end, is Cupid's arrow. When true love strikes, there's no turning back—not for Shawna and Parker, her fiance, who doesn't even remember that he's engaged; not for Annabella and Terry, who live in completely different worlds; not for Summer and Cabe who can't forget their teenage love. Holly and Steven were never meant to fall in love—Holly was supposed to get a juicy story, not a marriage proposal, from the famous bachelor. And our last two couples for the month are probably the most unlikely matches of all—strangers thrown together for a night who can't resist Cupid's arrow and turn an evening of romance into a lifetime of love!

We're very pleased to introduce Susan Crose to you this month. With **THE BRASS RING,** she's making her debut as a LOVESWEPT author—and what a sparkling debut it is! Be on the lookout for the beautiful cover on this book—it's our first bride and groom in a long time!

THE BRASS RING, LOVESWEPT #264, opens on the eve of Shawna McGuire's and Parker Harrison's wedding day when it seems that nothing can mar their perfect joy and anticipation on becoming husband and wife. But there's a terrible accident, and Shawna is left waiting at the church. Shawna almost loses her man, but she never gives up, and finally they do get to say their vows. This is a story about falling in love with the same person twice, and what could be more romantic than that?

Joan Elliott Pickart's **THE ENCHANTING MISS ANNABELLA,** LOVESWEPT #265, is such an enchanting love story that I guarantee you won't want to put this book down. Miss Annabella is the librarian in Harmony, Oklahoma, and Terry Russell is a gorgeous, blue-eyed, ladykiller pilot who has returned to the tiny town to visit his folks. All the ladies in Harmony fantasize about handsome Terry Russell, but Annabella doesn't even know what a fantasy is! Annabella's a late bloomer, and Terry is the

(continued)

one who helps her to blossom. Terry sees the woman hidden inside, and he falls in love with her. Annabella discovers herself, and then she can return Terry's love. When that happens, it's a match made in heaven!

FLYNN'S FATE, by Patt Bucheister, LOVESWEPT #266, is another example of this author's skill in touching our emotions. Summer Roberts loves the small town life and doesn't trust Cabe Flynn, the city slicker who lives life in Chicago's fast lane. Cabe was her teenage heartthrob, but years ago he gave up on Clearview and on Summer. Now he's back to claim his legacy, and Summer finds she can't bear to spend time with him because he awakens a sweet, wild hunger in her. Cabe wants to explore the intense attraction between them; he won't ignore his growing desire. He knows his own mind, and he also knows that Summer is his destiny—and with moonlight sails and words of love, he shows her this truth.

In **MADE FOR EACH OTHER** by Doris Parmett, LOVESWEPT #267, it's our heroine Holly Anderson's job to get an exclusive interview from LA's most eligible bachelor. Steven Chadwick guards his privacy so Holly goes undercover to get the scoop. She has no problem getting to know the gorgeous millionaire—in fact, he becomes her best friend and constant companion. Steven is too wonderful for words, and too gorgeous to resist, and Holly knows she must come clean and risk ruining their relationship. When friendly hugs turn into sizzling embraces, Holly gives up her story to gain his love. Best friends become best lovers! Doris Parmett is able to juggle all the elements of this story and deliver a wonderfully entertaining read.

STRICTLY BUSINESS by Linda Cajio, LOVESWEPT #268, maybe should have been titled, "Strictly Monkey Business". That describes the opening scene where Jess Brannen and Nick Mikaris wake up in bed together, scarcely having set eyes on each other before! They are both victims of a practical joke.

Things go from bad to worse when Jess shows up for a job interview and finds Nick behind the desk. They can't seem to stay away from each other, and Nick can't

(continued)

forget his image of her in that satin slip! Jess keeps insisting that she won't mix business with pleasure, even when she has the pleasure of experiencing his wildfire kisses. She doth protest too much—and finally her "no" becomes a "yes." This is Linda Cajio's sixth book for LOVESWEPT, and I know I speak for all your fans when I say, "Keep these wonderful stories coming, Linda!"

One of your favorite LOVESWEPT authors, Helen Mittermeyer, has a new book this month, and it's provocatively—and appropriately!—titled **ABLAZE,** LOVESWEPT #269. Heller Blane is a stunning blond actress working double shifts because she's desperately in need of funds. But is she desperate enough to accept $10,000 from a mysterious stranger *just* to have dinner with him? Conrad Wendell is dangerously appealing, and Heller is drawn to him. When their passionate night is over, she makes her escape, but Conrad cannot forget her. He's fallen in love with his vanished siren—she touched his soul—and he won't be happy until she's in his arms again. Thank you, Helen, for a new LOVESWEPT. **ABLAZE** has set our hearts on fire!

The HOMETOWN HUNK CONTEST is coming! We promised you entry blanks this month, but due to scheduling changes, the contest will officially begin next month. Just keep your eyes open for the magnificent men in your own hometown, then learn how to enter our HOMETOWN HUNK CONTEST *next month.*

Happy reading!

Sincerely,

Carolyn Nichols

Carolyn Nichols
  Editor
LOVESWEPT
Bantam Books
666 Fifth Avenue
New York, NY 10103

OFFICIAL DELANEYS, THE UNTAMED YEARS
MISSISSIPPI QUEEN° RIVERBOAT CRUISE
SWEEPSTAKES RULES

1. NO PURCHASE NECESSARY. Enter by completing the Official Entry Form below (or print your name, address, date of birth and telephone number on a plain 3" x 5" card) and send to:

> Bantam Books
> Delaneys, THE UNTAMED YEARS Sweepstakes
> Dept. HBG
> 666 Fifth Avenue
> New York, NY 10103

2. One Grand Prize will be awarded. There will be no prize substitutions or cash equivalents permitted. Grand Prize is a 7-night riverboat cruise for two on the luxury steamboat, The Mississippi Queen. Double occupancy accommodations, meals and on-board entertainment included. Round trip airfare provided by Reliable Travel International, Inc. (Estimated retail value $5,500.00. Exact value depends on actual point of departure.)

3. All entries must be postmarked and received by Bantam Books no later than August 1, 1988. The winner, chosen by random drawing, will be announced and notified by November 30, 1988. Trip must be completed by December 31, 1989, and is subject to space availability determined by Delta Queen Steamboat Company, and airline space availability determined by Reliable Travel International. If the Grand Prize winner is under 21 years of age on August 1, 1988, he/she must be accompanied by a parent or guardian. Taxes on the prize are the sole responsibility of the winner. Odds of winning depend on the number of completed entries received. Enter as often as you wish, but each entry must be mailed separately. Bantam Books is not responsible for lost, misdirected or incomplete entries.

4. The sweepstakes is open to residents of the U.S. and Canada, except the Province of Quebec, and is void where prohibited by law. If the winner is a Canadian he/she will be required to correctly answer a skill question in order to receive the prize. All federal, state and local regulations apply. Employees of Reliable Travel International, The Delta Queen Steamboat Co., and Bantam, Doubleday, Dell Publishing Group, Inc., their subsidiary and affiliates, and their immediate families are ineligible to enter.

5. The winner may be required to submit an Affidavit of Eligibility and Promotional Release supplied by Bantam Books. The winner's name and likeness may be used for publicity purposes without additional compensation.

6. For an extra copy of the Official Rules and Entry Form, send a self-addressed stamped envelope (Washington and Vermont Residents need not affix postage) by June 15, 1988 to:

> Bantam Books
> Delaneys, THE UNTAMED YEARS Sweepstakes
> Dept. HBG
> 666 Fifth Avenue
> New York, NY 10103

- -

OFFICIAL ENTRY FORM
DELANEYS, THE UNTAMED YEARS
MISSISSIPPI QUEEN° RIVERBOAT CRUISE SWEEPSTAKES

Name _____

Address _____

City _____ State _____ Zip Code _____

SW10